JASE

SMOKEJUMPERS

BOOK THREE

BY EVE RILEY

JASE

SMOKEJUMPERS

BOOK THREE

COPYRIGHT © 2023

EVE RILEY

ISBN: 978-1-77357-589-6

978-1-77357-590-2

PUBLISHED BY NAUGHTY NIGHTS PRESS LLC

COVER ART BY WILLSIN ROWE

DEAR READER

While many readers say my books are often dark and gritty, and that may be true, I also think they contain realistic themes that plague us in every day life. Which is why I would like to mention that *Jase* may contain some scenes that could be a trigger or very uncomfortable for some readers.

If you need to skip those memories, please do.

The descriptions of some historical incidents in this book are graphic and detailed. This is necessary to ensure readers understand the effect bullying can have on a person's psyche, often leading them to make less than positive life choices, and the consequences of those actions can last a lifetime.

In this story and in real life, both main characters spent several years in therapy to overcome their respective issues, even though I have skipped those formative years in the book. I contemplated starting from their teen years, but when I began writing I found the traumatic and horrible ruminations of such a childhood too much. I can only imagine how hard it was to actually live through it, so my utmost kudos go out to these men and the many more like them.

Could I have crafted this story without the details I did include, the memories of Jase and Quinn both? Probably. But the impact wouldn't have been the same, in my humble opinion, and the person for whom the memories were written for deserves to have his story told, even if it is in a fictional manner.

I would like to take the opportunity to encourage anyone who is being bullied, or suffering suicidal ideations, or for *any* reason whatsoever is in need, to seek out help. Someone does care.

Support is available 24 hours a day, 7 days a week through 9-8-8: Suicide Crisis Helpline.

Help is also available through Kids Help Phone (1-800-668-6868) and the Hope for Wellness Help Line (1-855-242-3310).

JASE

A bully redeemed. A truth revealed.
A new sizzling connection.

Quinn Sanders grew up in a strict and religious family, unable to be true to himself as a gay teen. Bullying was his coping mechanism, but his regrets are many. He became a New Orleans firefighter as a means of redemption for his past.

After a horrific fire leaves him the only survivor of the station house, another kind of guilt now plagues his every waking moment. Back in Baton Rouge for a fresh start, Quinn finds the past rearing its ugly head once more.

Jase Turner joined the fire department to fit society's expectations of masculinity. After a childhood filled with bullying, life-altering choices, and years of therapy, Jase is still terrified of anyone discovering he is gay.

When Quinn transfers to Jase's station, the old feelings of animosity resurface, causing tension in the firehouse. Forced to work closely, the two men discover they have more in common than they could have imagined and Jase starts to see Quinn in a whole new light.

Will they be able to overcome their history and give in to the intense emotional connection they now have?

CHAPTER ONE

Quinn

I STOOD THERE, the deafening roar of the flames drowning out everything else. The older warehouse loomed above us, a monstrous entity swallowing the night. My fellow firefighters, a band of brothers and sisters, geared up beside me. We exchanged nods, words stolen by the crackling inferno before us.

"Sanders, you ready for this?" Captain Hagan shouted, his voice muffled by the mask that obscured his face. I nodded, the weight of my gear comforting in its familiarity.

We charged into the heat, a relentless wall of fire waiting to consume us. Smoke stung my eyes as we pushed forward, our hoses spitting defiance against the red fury. My helmet shielded my face from the intense heat, but sweat soaked my clothes as we advanced through the orange haze. The embers danced like fireflies, and the air was thick with the acrid scent of burning wood, a reminder of the unforgiving challenge ahead.

I swallowed the harsh taste of fear, a veritable lump in my throat as we trudged through the powerful flames toward the center. Black smoke clung to the air like a shroud as we pushed forward, the red fury rolling through the room feeling even hotter now. Adrenaline surged through my veins, pushing back the almost all consuming panic that threatened to take my knees out from under me with each step.

I could do this. Had done so more times than I could count. I breathed the warm oxygen through the mask. In, out, in... the repetitive motions calming my thudding heart, centering me, if only a little.

The building groaned and shifted, its walls creaking in protest. My radio suddenly crackled to life, the voices echoing, overlapping with urgency.

"We need backup on the west side! It's spreading too fast!" I heard the voice of my teammate, Irving Jessop, crackle through the airwaves.

"Roger that! Hold if you can, Jessop!" Captain Hagen shouted into his radio, his silhouette a beacon in the darkness mere steps in front of me.

We fought, not only against the fire but against time itself. My heart raced, adrenaline coursing through my veins as I swung my axe, smashing through obstacles and punching through fire-brittle walls in our path. The heat was relentless, a punishing force that tested the limits of our ability.

"Sanders, watch your back!" shouted Jakes, one of the newer recruits. I turned just in time to see a flaming beam hurtling toward us. Instinct kicked in, and I pushed Jakes out of harm's way, the beam crashing down with a shower of sparks behind me, the rush of sound, almost a physical force, overwhelming my eardrums.

The warehouse seemed to breathe, a living entity with a desire to consume us. The walls shuddered, and panic gripped the air.

"We gotta get out, now!" Captain Hagan's order cut through the chaos.

Retreating was a battle in itself. Smoke thickened, visibility reduced to shadows dancing in the haze. My lungs burned, each breath a reminder of the peril we faced. The sound of creaking beams overhead sent a chill down my spine.

"Move, move, move!" Captain Hagan screamed into the darkness, the creaks and groans of the beams now reaching a fever pitch that made my ears ring.

We stumbled back, racing to retrace our earlier path toward the door, toward freedom, the fire chasing us like a relentless predator. The world became a blur of orange and black, and I felt the building shudder beneath my feet.

Then it happened—the deafening roar, the ground trembling and then heaving beneath my boots, everything around me became a moving maze of broken footings and charred obstructions.

I turned, horror gripping my chest as the warehouse crumbled, a cascade of fiery chaos sucking the very breath from my lungs. The flames licked at my heels as I sprinted for the flashing lights visible just through door, a desperate escape from the collapsing nightmare.

The air was thick with ash, and my heart pounded in my ears. I emerged from the inferno, coughing and gasping for air. I turned back to witness the once-mighty structure reduced to a smoldering ruin. The guttural roar of the fire had silenced, replaced by the crackling of embers.

The realization hit me like a physical blow—my comrades, my brothers and sisters, gone. A lump formed in my throat, and my hands trembled as I surveyed the devastation. The weight of my survival pressed heavy on my shoulders, a guilt that threatened to consume me.

CHAPTER TWO

Quinn

THE FLICKERING GLOW of the television illuminated the dim room, casting shadows that danced along the walls. The remote felt heavy in my hand as I hesitated to press play. I punched the button and the news anchor's voice filled the stony silence, a voice that seemed too cheery for the story it carried.

"Breaking news in New Orleans tonight. A devastating warehouse fire claimed the lives of several firefighters. The blaze erupted late last night, turning the structure into an inferno that raged for hours. The cause of the fire is still under investigation."

The images on the screen painted a vivid picture of the chaos I had left behind. The orange glow of the flames, the billowing smoke, the silhouettes of firefighters battling an enemy that cared nothing for mercy. My comrades, my brothers, their faces frozen in time on the screen.

I felt the lump in my throat grow, an ache that mirrored the pain in my chest. The news report continued, listing the names of the fallen, of the men and women in my company, on my shift—

people who had become friends in my time at the firehouse—each mention like a hammer striking my heart. Hagen, Jakes, Jessop, MacDonald, Ramirez, Kramer. Their images flashed on the screen—faces etched with determination, smiles that echoed in the recesses of my memory.

Survivor's guilt clawed at me, an invisible weight that threatened to crush my spirit. A tear slipped down my cheek, and I wiped it away angrily, as if the physical act could erase the emotional turmoil within me.

The newscast moved on to interviews with grieving families, the raw pain evident in their eyes. I watched, a silent spectator to the aftermath of a tragedy I had somehow escaped. The remorse weighed heavier with each passing moment, my breaths becoming shallow, my chest constricting, the pressure building as I grappled with the harsh reality.

I reached out to the screen, fingers grazing the faces frozen in time. "I'm so sorry," the words slipped from my lips, a whisper lost in the stillness of the room. The ache in my chest intensified, overwhelming me and stealing my breath from my lungs just as the heat and flames had right before the world had crumpled around me, and I opened my mouth in a silent scream that echoed inside my head.

The room seemed to close in around me, the walls pressing in as if trying to suffocate the responsibility and sorrow that clung to my soul. I punched the remote, shutting off the television and plunging the room into darkness once more. The silence was deafening, broken only by the distant wail of a siren, a haunting reminder of the world outside.

I sat amidst the shadows, my mind a storm of emotions—grief, guilt, and a profound sense of loss. The weight of my survival bore down on me like a heavy cloak, and the faces on the screen lingered in the shadows, with accusing eyes that only I could see.

In that moment, the room felt colder than the night of the inferno. The flames may have taken the warehouse, but the fire within me continued to burn, fueled by the memories of those who would never return.

The days that followed the blaze were a blur of debriefings and condolences. Sleep came fitfully, haunted by the screams and the inferno's roar. Each face, each laugh, now a ghost that danced in the shadows

EVE RILEY

of my mind.

CHAPTER THREE

Quinn

A WEEK LATER, my livingroom remained shrouded in darkness, the blackout curtains closed tightly over the large windows, a silent sanctuary where my thoughts echoed over and over in my mind, louder than any spoken words would be. The faces of my fallen coworkers lingered behind my eyelids, flashing back at me on repeat, their spirits cast as shadows on the walls, tormenting me each time I opened my eyes. I could almost hear their voices in the stillness, their laughter and camaraderie haunting the air.

The weight of the guilt bore down on me, an oppressive force that threatened to break me. I couldn't escape the relentless questions that echoed in my mind on repeat.

Why me?

Why was I the one who walked away while they became memories etched in the ashes?

I reclined on the couch in my unwashed state, my hair and skin greasy and a foul stench emanating from my skin, the remains of beer bottles and empty food containers littering nearly every square inch in the filth that was now my apartment.

The silence of the room was broken by the distant wail of another passing siren, a reminder that life still continued outside my dark cocoon. I sucked in a deep breath, the air feeling thick and heavy in my lungs. The room seemed to close in around me, and I stood, needing to escape the suffocating stillness.

I paced the room, running a hand through my hair as if trying to grasp hold of something tangible. The images from the news report replayed in my mind—as they had a dozen times or more each day since—the flames, the collapsing structure, the faces of my brothers and sisters frozen in a moment of despair. The guilt twisted in my gut, a relentless knot that refused to loosen its grip.

A framed photograph caught my eye, nestled among the clutter on a shelf. It was a picture of us, the firefighting crew, taken on a day when the sun shone bright, and laughter echoed in the air. I traced the contours of each face with my fingertips, a bittersweet connection to the past.

"I'm sorry," I whispered again, the words barely audible in the murky room. The stark and silent walls seemed to absorb the confession, offering no solace in return. The photograph became a relic, a portal to a time when we were invincible, untouchable by the harsh reality that had unfolded.

As I gazed at the faces frozen in the frame, anger and determination sparked within me. I couldn't change the past, couldn't undo the choices that led to the

JASE

tragic outcome, but I could honor their
memory. The guilt remained, a scar
etched on my tortured soul, but perhaps,
in honoring their legacy, I could find a
way to carry the weight.

A sudden beep pierced the silence,
pulling me from my reverie. I glanced at
my phone, and an email notification
flashed on the screen. The subject line
caught my attention like an icy cold slap,
cutting through the haze of my grief.

"Transfer Notice: Firehouse 21."

The words stared back at me, and a
bitter taste settled in my mouth.

With a heavy sigh, I opened the email.
The words unfolded before me, a new
chapter waiting to be written. Firehouse
21, a fresh start in a city that held both
memories and a potential prospects. The
dark room, once suffocating, now seemed

to expand, to lighten just a little as a gentle breeze rippled the edge of curtain open just a sliver, allowing the bright sunlight from outside to pierce the gloom, offering a glimpse of a future yet to be defined.

A fresh start, it said.

A chance to heal.

Firehouse 21.

A new chapter, a new team.

Hope bloomed in my chest for a brief moment.

But could returning to Baton Rouge, my hometown, truly be a new start for me?

I'd fled the city years ago in an attempt to escape from the life I'd led there, and I'd succeeded. I'd started anew in New Orleans already.

Was there even another chance for me

to get it right this time?

Did I even deserve another chance?

Doubt dampened the optimism that had only moments ago raced through my veins like a light in a pitch-black tunnel.

I sighed, staring at the screen, the cursor blinking like a relentless reminder of the past. I wasn't even entirely sure I was ready for this, to return to work, but the mandated psychiatrist had cleared me for duty after only three appointments, so what did I know. Maybe I was as good at fooling him as I was at fooling myself into believing I was okay.

My outlook on so many things had changed recently, the reflection of what could have happened to me in that fire bringing clarity to my mind for the first time in my entire life. Clarity and so much regret. I needed to do better from here on in, *be* better. Maybe I wouldn't make up for all the transgressions of my past, for surviving where all my peers had perished, but I would sure as hell try to make my future something I could be proud of.

I pocketed the phone, the glow of its screen a beacon in the darkness. The shadows of the fallen firefighters lingered, but in that moment, a spark of resilience ignited within me. I had to try. The guilt would remain, but I would carry it forward, a silent tribute to those who could no longer walk beside me.

As I stepped into the bathroom to wash away the filth on my body, to prepare for the tentative future, the shadows in the dark seemed to recede, replaced by a flicker of hope that refused to be extinguished. Firehouse Twenty-One awaited, a new canvas where the echoes of the past and a strong desire to become a better man might just bring redemption and the possibility of a future.

Little did I know, that transfer to Firehouse Twenty-One would thrust me into a world of facing more of my past and thus, future challenges far beyond the flames I had left behind.

CHAPTER FOUR

Jase

"YO, TURNER! YOU actually going to drink that or just stare at it until you fall in it?"

The deep voice pulled me out of the vacant void I stared into without realizing it. I looked up at the guy who was only a year or two younger than me with shaved blond hair, which he could keep up with at home, blue eyes, and a smile that was much too bright for me right now.

My name is actually Jase, but my coworker, Mark, insists on calling people by their last names. Mark Rollins was an interesting guy. Although he never joined any of the out-of-work socials, he was recognized as a good man with a good sense of humor. He was fun to work with and was always the first to make something into a game when the atmosphere got too heavy around the fire station or out on the trucks.

But not even his chirpy attitude could lift my spirits after the three weeks of night shifts. I hated them. Not only did you never see the sun apart from when you went home and tried to sleep, but there were only two extremes of events that occurred even in a city as large and as busy as Baton Rouge. Either everything happened, and there was barely any time to have a breather, or nothing happened, and the minutes just dragged. We were the most central station, so we often got called for most of the events in the city, but there were still plenty of quiet nights where nothing really happened. Sure, on those nights, it was possible to catch some sleep in the bunks, but they weren't comfortable, and the sounds of the station around you would keep everyone awake.

"How the hell do you still have the energy right now?" I asked incredulously. Part of me almost thought he was magic for his energy levels.

Night shifts were usually twelve hours, and it was always four days on, three days off. But at the end of the fourth day, everybody's spirits were always low, and I was constantly irritable. I knew I shouldn't be, or at least I should mask it enough so my colleagues didn't bear the brunt of it, but I couldn't help it. I had never been one to deal well with a lack of sleep.

Still, not even the crappy night shifts every few months could make me think about quitting. I loved my job. It kept me fit and alert, and there was a real feeling of pride when I got back to the station after a fire or during the day when people smiled a little brighter when I told them my occupation. I am slightly more slender than the average firefighter, but that means I get to be an inspiration for all the smaller kids out there who might like the idea of this. I found it was a job where you were admired for the masculinity of it without having to be toxic in the way you portray yourself.

Mark laughed brightly and let his shoulders roll in a shrug. "I have a newborn at home. I'm a pro at functioning on no sleep!"

"What was your excuse before the baby?" Johnson called across the room.

"I got loads of sex!" Mark barked a laugh.

Everyone else laughed aloud at that statement. "Yeah, right," I laughed. "She blue balled you so often, even Captain Rouke got more than you, and he's getting divorced."

Laughter rippled through the crew as Mark shrugged without argument. I decided not to point out that, like everybody else here, Mark had been one to fall asleep in every nook and cranny of the station. It was impossible to do four twelve-hour shifts in a row at night and not doze off when it was lacking in excitement. So long as you did your grunt work and kept your equipment clean and ready, none of the team gave each other hassle for it.

Still, he must be doing something right as Mark was the only one not sitting cradling a coffee like a lifeline as the clock ticked closer and closer to the nine o'clock point, which would allow him to go home and crash.

That was all I could think about. My fresh double bed, still in shadow from blackout curtains, and maybe if I was lucky, the cat who visited from time to time would come in for a snooze.

Unfortunately, it seemed like we would need more time to be able to vanish as soon as the clock struck nine that day. At ten to the hour, the station's Captain walked into the room, and immediately everyone went quiet, hoping there wouldn't be some situation that kept us all here on overtime.

"Morning, everyone," Captain Clarke spoke with a deep voice and an energy he would not be getting returned at this time of the day. He didn't take any notice of the tired mumbles he received in return before continuing. "We've got a new recruit to introduce who will be working your shift patterns. Figured the extra set of young hands would be very helpful since Trevor recently retired. He's been part of the team over in New Orleans, so he knows what he is doing and should be a wonderful asset."

A ripple of relief washed through the

team. I could feel it in waves from my closest friends here. Trevor had been a good worker even with his older age, and losing him had left everyone feeling a little spread thin during their hours here. If they had found someone who was already good at the job in general, it would take off a lot of pressure.

A man walked in behind the Captain, and frankly, I had to be very careful to control my expression. At this stage of my life, I was an expert at hiding my attraction to other men, but this man was stunning. He must have stood at nearly six foot three, a good three inches taller than myself; I had always liked a man who was taller than me, and the idea of being able to curl into someone's arms was always my biggest secret. His shirt did nothing to hide the firmness of the muscles that molded his shoulders and chest into something that was difficult not to stare at.

It was his face that really drew me in, though. He had a solid, strong jawline with a very slight dusting of stubble where he hadn't quite gotten close enough with a wet shave earlier that morning. Short, near-black hair was styled into a messy shag toward the front, just long enough to bury fingers into and get a slight grip of. Plump lips with a healthy pink hue to them and deep green eyes sitting under severe brows.

Fuck me.

The man's gaze met mine, and I froze. A dash of brown over his right eye, and though small, the birthmark was unmistakable and something I recognized immediately. Dread, anxiety, and anger pooled in my stomach as I vaguely listened to the Captain's introduction.

"This is Quinn Sanders. He's joining me today to learn the ropes of this place specifically compared to his last station, then it's up to you lot to make sure he settles enough to be good as he was before."

Shit.

It was really *him*.

Quinn Sanders was one of my biggest bullies back in high school. He made my life a living hell... and now here he was, tall, handsome, charming smile.

Fucking dick.

Sure, I wasn't a shabby deal myself. But that didn't stop me from immediately becoming self-conscious as I compared myself to him. It wasn't fair that someone who was such an asshole as a kid could

JASE

grow up to look like that.

I could not help but scowl a little as I watched Quinn move around the room and introduce himself to the team. Johnson gave me a raised eyebrow when he noticed my expression, but with a shake of my head, I knew he understood that I would explain another time.

"Word of warning, don't drink the coffee. It tastes like shit," I said as he stepped over to shake my hand, placing my half-empty coffee in his extended hand and walking past him without another word. I needed sleep or alcohol right now, probably both if the memories of a young Quinn surfacing had anything to say about it.

CHAPTER FIVE

Jase

THE MEMORIES ASSAULTED me like it hadn't been over fifteen years, reminding me of the horrors of my days in high school and sucking the breath from my lungs.

The school hallway buzzed with the chaotic energy of passing students. Lockers slammed shut, laughter echoed, and the air was thick with anticipation. I navigated through the crowd, trying to stay inconspicuous, but I could feel Quinn's predatory gaze following my every move.

"Look who's here, guys! It's Jase the loser!" Quinn's voice cut through the clamor, drawing the attention of the onlookers. He approached, flanked by his loyal followers, a menacing grin etched across his face.

"What's up, Jase? Still thinking you belong here?" Quinn taunted, his words dripping with disdain. The hallway became a narrow alley with no escape, and the air grew heavy with tension.

I kept my head down, trying to ignore him, but Quinn wasn't one to be ignored. He shoved me, and I stumbled against the lockers, the metal biting into my back. The metallic taste of fear surged in my mouth, and I bit down on my bottom lip to suppress it. I knew if I showed him my fear it would only spur him on, make things worse than they already were.

"Pathetic," Quinn spat, his cronies snickering behind him. "You're always in the way, Jase. Can't you take a hint and disappear? Like, die already, dude. You're nothing but a waste of space and you know it."

The hallway seemed to close in around me as Quinn's aggression escalated. He grabbed the collar of my shirt, yanking me forward until our faces were inches apart. The stench of his overpowering cologne mingled with the metallic tang of my own blood. I focused in on the small brown birthmark over his right eye, determined to keep my mouth shut, trying desperately to *avoid speaking or any sudden movements, anything that might set him off more.*

"You think you're tough, huh? You're nothing but a fucking queer," Quinn sneered, punctuating each word with a cruel shove that sent me staggering backward. The taste of copper intensified, and I wiped my mouth, trying to hide the evidence of his attack.

Emotion swirled within me—a toxic blend of shame, anger, and helplessness. Quinn's belittling remarks echoed in my ears, each insult carving a deeper wound inside me as if he had taken a knife and twisted it in my gut. The physical pain mirrored the emotional turmoil that filled my chest, heavy and debilitating, making me wonder if what he said was true.

I was a waste of space, wasn't I?

No one liked me. I could never do

anything right so why would they?

I had no friends, no one I could go to who would understand how I felt and take me seriously. So why did I continue to bother?

My parents, as good of parents as they may be, or at least tried to be, just didn't understand me. They were convinced it was just a phase and I would outgrow it soon.

The bell rang, signaling the end of the torment, this time anyway. Quinn and his cronies dispersed, leaving me leaning against the lockers, battered and bruised. The hallway returned to its frenetic pace, but the echoes of Quinn's cruelty lingered, a painful melody that refused to fade. I sucked in a deep breath, swallowing the blood-tinged taste of defeat.

CHAPTER SIX

Quinn

MY FIRST DAY on the job in my hometown had not started the way I had hoped. I watched the light brown-haired man walk away before looking down at the cup he had left in my hand. The liquid inside was black and thick, like tar. A shiver ran up my spine when his eyes met mine from across the room before he walked from the room.

What the hell?

What kind of greeting was that?

"That's Jase Turner, don't mind him. He can get pretty grouchy by the end of a three week stint on nights," the Captain said to me. Though I knew that wasn't what I had just witnessed.

His name was all the explanation I needed.

He had grown up for sure. Jase had been a weedy little kid at school whose life I had made a living hell. He wasn't the only one, but I had picked on him enough to remember him vividly. I hated myself for who I used to be, I wanted to make things right, but I suspected that wouldn't be so easy having to work with Jase. He clearly had not forgotten me or forgiven my actions.

JASE

Deciding to keep that to myself for now, I forced a smile onto my face and nodded along with the Captain's brief description of the team I would be working on. It sounded like they were a close-knit group of guys who trusted each other, there was only one female, Carmen Diaz, but she could run rings around every other person there. Still, if they were all so close, it could pose some problems fitting in.

The station was more significant than the one I was used to in New Orleans, but it was self-explanatory. Everything was generally kept in similar places that I would logically look at when searching for that specific item or piece of equipment. At least that made it easier for me to ponder what I was going to do about the Jase situation.

If I hadn't known him in the past, he was precisely the type of man I would ask out on a date. His jaw was softly rounded, and his brown eyes were gentle and kind. He had a slight mop of styled hair on his head, which I would have adored to make a mess out of. His nose was straight, but not too long or wide. And he had dimples.

Dimples!

He had the kind of face that most girls dreamed about; one that made their stomachs flutter when they saw him. Of course, I was no girl... but that didn't make him any less gorgeous.

I shook those thoughts out of my head pretty quickly. I would be lucky if Jase didn't hate me enough to convince the Captain to move me to another team, let alone appreciate me checking him out and damn near drooling.

JASE

The day didn't take as long as I feared it might after the revelation of who I would be working with.

The fire station was central to a lot of Baton Rouge, so even as I walked out of the front doors that evening, the streets were bustling with students, commuters, and groups of people meeting for a social life I had not yet experienced in this town. It wasn't as lit up and as mystical as New Orleans had sometimes been as the sun began to set, but there was still a sense of pride in the town. There was little graffiti to be found, and a lot of the shops on the walk back to where I was staying were independent and quirky, reminiscent of old-time family businesses that most cities were in the process of destroying with their chain stores.

On the way home, I stopped at the

small eccentric coffee shop just around the corner from home. Ordering a large, unhealthy frappe and a double espresso, I couldn't help but chuckle to myself that Jase had been right. The coffee available at the station was utterly god awful and should be illegal.

I sipped at my espresso as I entered the apartment I was staying in. As my parents were still highly God-fearing and I was openly out as a gay man, when I moved back to town, I had figured that it would be easier for all of us if I weren't around constantly. Thankfully, an old friend had come to my aid.

Jared Linwood was someone I knew from school, not one of my peer group, and therefore someone who also ended up bullying alongside me, but an older student who actually kept me from becoming worse than I was. He kept me away from the temptation of drugs and smoking when my peers had started to turn to them. He was like an older brother, and since coming back to town, I was crashing with him.

I would forever be glad for Jared in my life, though I often wished I had been smart enough to listen to all his advice, like now. If I had listened more back then, perhaps I wouldn't have bullied others so much in order to cover my own fears and insecurities... And then maybe I wouldn't be facing the predicament I was in.

But I'd learned and accepted a long time ago that you couldn't change the past. Hell, you couldn't even change other people. The only thing I had any control over was myself and how I lived my life.

"Hey! Awesome!" Jared chirped up as

he saw the frappe I held out to him. "What did I do to deserve this? Or do you want something?" He raised an eyebrow at me and laughed. In the past, I had had a major crush on him for his free attitude, but that had faded over time... and with the knowledge that he was straight and his high school sweetheart would always be the love of his life even if she was always traveling abroad with her work.

"Why do you assume I want something?" I laughed.

"Because I know you."

I shook my head with a slight chuckle as I plopped down on the sofa beside Jared. "I just wanted to ask for some advice," I admitted after a moment.

"See. I know you." Jared laughed, taking a long sip of his frappe before leaning into the back of the sofa and looking at me through his floppy blond fringe. "Go on then, what's up? Bad first day?"

"Not exactly. The Captain was cool, and the team seemed like a close-knit group," I started.

"So... what's the problem?" Jared asked.

"Do you remember a kid at school called Jase Turner?"

"Should I?" Jared raised an eyebrow at me.

Shrugging softly, I leaned back and took a couple more gulps of my espresso. "I suppose not." I sighed. "He was one of the kids I gave hell to..."

"Ah... He's a fireman now?" Jared hadn't taken long to figure that out. I nodded slowly.

"Yeah. And on my new team. And, by

the look of it, he remembers me and is not pleased about my arrival," I explained.

"He said that?"

"Didn't need to. I grew up in a highly religious environment and came out as gay. I know what revulsion looks like." Though his disgust was much more understandable and something I didn't know how to work with.

"Well, there's not a lot you can do about what happened," Jared started, mulling over a mouthful of frappe.

"I could apologize to him," I suggested.

"Is that to make him feel better, or you?"

"Huh?"

"Well, he might not want to acknowledge it. He might still need to be angry to heal from it," Jared mused.

I understood what he meant. It wasn't

that anger needed to be out loud, but the anger that could be felt after being mistreated was the part of yourself that knew you deserved better, and learning to accept and deal with that anger in a healthy way was a big step in healing.

I had learned that in the first couple of years away from home.

"What you can do is just show him that you have changed." Jared smiled, though he quickly laughed when I looked at him with confusion. "You know, be a good guy. Work hard. Show you respect him. All that jazz. And if he ever brings up the topic of school, you let him say his piece before you say yours. He's the one who was tormented by you. It ain't his fault you were internally tormented by family and religion."

I let my head flop back onto the back

of the sofa, looking up at the magnolia-colored ceiling. "Yeah, I suppose you're right."

I would have much preferred to make things right immediately, but there was also an excellent chance that Jase was expecting me to still be as horrible as I used to be. If there was any chance of forgiveness, he would need to believe I was no longer a danger to his physical or mental health.

"So, what about the rest of the place? Think you'll be cool there?" Jared asked, turning the conversation to the job itself.

"Oh yeah. Bigger than my last station, but that should mean it's better stocked and has the proper manpower." I smiled lightly before glancing at him as Jared clapped me on the shoulder.

"I'm proud of you for getting back to

it," he said almost cryptically, knowing the reason I left New Orleans wasn't my favorite topic. "You're doing good, kid."

"Dude. I'm a year younger than you," I protested with a laugh, shoving his hand away.

"And don't you ever forget that that makes me the wise old sage here."

"Senile, more like it."

With the atmosphere much lighter and my head not buried in concerns and regrets, it was easy to let myself relax properly for the evening.

By the time I headed to bed, three beers and a good healthy amount of meat lovers pizza later, I at least had an idea of how to present myself at work after the first few introduction shifts.

CHAPTER SEVEN

Jase

"COME ON, CAP. Can't you just stick him on another team?" I pleaded as my first port of call the moment I walked into the station a few days later.

I had spent the last few days stewing on the fact that Quinn Sanders was joining my team at work. The mere idea of it had me drinking extra and gave me anxiety-like jitters.

Back in school, he had been one of the tall good-looking guys from a good respectable family. His father was a preacher, and so he always turned the other way whenever Quinn's victims were what he deemed as sinners. Quinn had always claimed that I was gay, and that was why he would torment me. He would call me slurs and laugh about how the bible claimed that a man who lay with another man should be stoned while throwing stones at me.

Even though I had never come out and still kept my sexuality a deep secret, his words and actions cut me deep. I wasn't manly enough back then to avoid such torture. I knew the present would be different, though. I had a masculine job, a larger and more manly body frame, my parents approved, and I could get any girl I wanted... but if Quinn was back, I was petrified that he would start back with the old comments. Comments that would make people realize that perhaps I wasn't as straight as I portrayed myself to be.

"I'm sorry, Jase, but you need the manpower more than any other team." Captain Clarke sighed. He didn't really understand; I couldn't share everything without outing myself either.

Fuck.

Imagine being in a job with very fit men and then them all suddenly discovering you were gay and hid it from them. I knew the Captain had come out as gay last year, as had Hawke and a couple others on both our shift and the second shift, but they were different. Cap wasn't on the line like I was but rather sat up in his office most of the time, Hawke had been super-popular since I'd started at the station so even though he'd never hidden that part of himself, no one was going to look down on him for it. Even if they did, it wasn't something Cap would tolerate in his house. I knew that, I did, but I was still convinced they would all get weird around me. They might think I perved on them when we got back from jobs and changed out of smoke-ridden clothes or might hit on them in the showers. I felt sick thinking about how they would look at me with judgment and disgust.

No. Keeping my secret was more important than getting the Captain to understand.

Leaving his office, I headed back to the main room, where we would wait for a call. It had some scruffy old sofas to sit on and a pool table. It also had a little gym area where the staff had pooled money together to get some weights and a treadmill. It wasn't much, but on quiet days, it was nice to do a little bit to keep active.

"Hey, man," Mark stepped over to me and held out a coffee bought from the shop across the road. I took it with a grumble about him being some kind of angel sent from above. Even with a newborn and lack of sleep, Mark was still thoughtful, and he knew how much I hated starting my day with the swill the coffee machine here served... and how I always woke up too late to stop off at a shop myself.

"Where have you been?" he asked, following me to the sofas and plonking himself down.

"Captain's office."

"Shit. Everything good?"

His immediate concern made me chuckle. I suspected that Mark would be one of the few here who I could tell everything, and he wouldn't judge, but I never had the guts to do it.

"Yeah. I just don't want that Sanders guy on the team."

"Why not?"

"Because he's a jackass that I went to school with who bullied people until they tried to kill themselves," I explained, leaving out the fact that one of those people was me. Though, the way Mark looked at me suggested I didn't need to say that part.

"You serious?" he asked.

"Yep. Never made any attempt to

change, and being the son of the preacher who taught at the stupidly religious school, he got away with everything." I shook my head.

"Fuck. Yeah, that's not good. If he was like that, he might even end up triggering people that we are trying to help," Mark mused, anger simmering in his eyes. He was a fairly righteous man. He often got into arguments with people who were discriminating, even without realizing it.

"Exactly. And this is the local area to that school... a lot of people will have known him," I said.

"There might even be people here who he tormented. There's a few from your school in the other teams, right?"

I nodded as he looked at me for confirmation.

The door opened across the room, and

the man in question walked in. Mark let a small hum leave his throat as we watched Quinn quietly greet Johnson, who was closest to the door.

"We'll keep an eye on him. Leave the rest to me," Mark commented, ignoring my raised eyebrow as he pushed himself to his feet and smiled.

"Quinn, just the man. Got a job for you and your giant height!" he chirped, seemingly as friendly as ever.

"Of course." Quinn nodded with a small smile on his lips, obviously put there to seem polite. A smile that somehow managed to stay there as Mark explained that the tops of all the lockers needed a good cleaning, but no one else was tall enough to do it.

I had been at the station for nearly ten years now, and I had never seen the top of the lockers cleaned. The cleaner who worked here was a tiny little lady who would have had no chance, so everyone had told her not to worry about them. The dust, dirt, spiders, and god knows what else, was something we just ignored. I almost laughed as Mark handed Quinn a pair of gloves and a bucket of hot water for the job.

I didn't expect Quinn to take to the job so easily or to actually do a full and excellent job without so much as a complaint.

The son of a preacher doing cleaning work happily?

Seemed unlikely. I suspected he was just putting on a front for the beginning of the job. At least by lunch, word had gotten around about what kind of man he was.

"Gotta ask, man..." Johnson nudged my shoulder as we cleaned up the equipment on truck fifty-seven. "Were you one of them?"

"What you talking about?"

"I saw the way you froze up when the Captain introduced him. You were one of the kids he bullied, right?"

I raised an eyebrow at the man who was still fresh-faced out of college but a damn good addition to the team. "Was I that obvious?"

"Nah, but me and my twin were bullied in school too, so I know the haunted look it can give you." He shrugged as though we weren't talking about something potentially very painful.

"Huh. Well, yeah, I was," I admitted. "I was a scrawny kid, and I still have a scar from one of those days." And some from the attempt I made to make all the pain end, but that would remain unsaid.

"I get it. If I had to work with my bully, I'd be all over the place. Puts the whole team at risk to be on edge like that." Johnson sighed.

I hadn't thought about it like that.

Damn.

That would have been a much better argument to take to the Captain. There was no way that I was about to trust Quinn with my life out in the field, and sometimes that was a level that was required. It could put my life in danger or someone else's. I pushed myself up to stand at my full height, planning on going back to the Captain's office when the alarm went off.

"Small stove fire on Fern Avenue. Get your asses there quick before it becomes a house fire!" the dispatcher called over the tannoy system as everyone on the team dropped what they were doing and ran for the gear.

Having a another member jump onto the trucks should have been a relief, but frankly, as I slid into the passenger seat next to Johnson with Mark sliding in on the back bench, and then watching as Quinn jumped into the other truck with Hawke, Carmen, Gage, and Zander, I couldn't help but feel on edge even for a routine job like this.

CHAPTER EIGHT

Jase

THE SUN HUNG low in the sky, casting long shadows across the courtyard. I trudged over the blacktop with my head down, backpack pulled tight against my shoulders, trying to make myself smaller, invisible. But high school had a way of amplifying everything, and I could feel his eyes on me before I even saw him.

A towering figure with a twisted grin, Quinn led his entourage straight toward me. Their laughter sliced through the air like a knife, and the scent of impending humiliation filled my nostrils. I tightened my grip on the straps of my backpack, bracing for impact.

"Well, well, look who we have here," Quinn sneered, his voice dripping with contempt. *"Jase, the eternal loser. How's it going, loser?"*

The acrid taste of bile rose in my throat as I tried to ignore the jabs, but Quinn wasn't one to be easily brushed off. He shoved me, sending my backpack sprawling across the concrete. Papers scattered like confetti, and the laughter around us intensified.

"Oops, clumsy Jase," Quinn mocked, his lackeys chuckling in agreement. *"Maybe*

you should stick to something you're good at, like being a total failure. Mommy's little gay boy, can't even be a man. More like a girl than anything else, eh, Jase? You like other boys, Jase? "

I clenched my jaw, feeling the sting of embarrassment burning on my cheeks. The metallic tang of blood filled my mouth as I bit down hard on my tongue.

"What's the matter, Jase? Cat got your tongue?" Quinn jeered, a wicked glint in his eyes. "Or maybe you're just too dumb to come up with a comeback."

The bell echoed through the courtyard, a cruel reminder that the torture would have to be cut short. But Quinn wasn't finished. He grabbed my backpack, dangling it high above his head like a trophy, while his lackeys closed in, forming a circle.

"Come on, Jase, reach for it," Quinn taunted, holding my belongings just out of reach. *"Unless you're too much of a wimp even for that."*

I could feel the frustration boiling within me, the desire to fight back clawing at my insides. But I held back, not wanting to give them the satisfaction.

"Look at him, guys! Jase is about to cry!" Quinn announced, his buddies erupting in laughter.

The scent of asphalt mixed with the bitter taste of defeat as I stood there, surrounded. Quinn finally dropped my backpack, but not before shoving me one last time. I stumbled backward, crashing into the chain-link fence. The metallic clang echoed in my ears, drowning out the laughter that followed me like a haunting melody.

JASE

As the bullies sauntered away, triumphant in their cruel victory, I collected my scattered belongings. The courtyard lay silent after the storm of humiliation, the laughter of Quinn and his cronies lingering like a persistent echo. Everything around me seemed colder, the world a little darker.

I sat alone against the cold, unforgiving bricks, shoulders slumped, backpack abandoned beside me. Blood pulsed in my temples, my body a canvas of pain from Quinn's relentless assaults. A bruised spirit, aching bones—a testament to my perpetual status as Quinn Sanders' punching bag.

The tinny tang of blood clung to the back of my throat, and I could feel the weight of hopelessness pressing down on me.

Why did I have to endure this day after day?

What had I done to deserve the constant torment?

As the darkness threatened to swallow me whole, a thought emerged, insidious and tempting. The idea of escaping it all, of finding solace in oblivion, crept into the corners of my mind. A desperate plea for an end to the suffering.

An idea formed as I climbed to my feet, hot tears tracking down my cheeks.

The sun dipped lower on the horizon, casting long shadows across the deserted courtyard as I made my way toward the path that led home.

I was so done.

CHAPTER NINE

Quinn

I WASN'T EXPECTING too much from my first day at work, but I wasn't sure I was expecting quite so much hazing. At least, it could have been seen as hazing. I suspected it was more than that, though. Usually, hazing was something that brought a few laughs and made the newcomer feel like an idiot for a brief moment, like asking them to go and find a skirting board ladder or ask the Captain for a long weight. They were small and daft tasks and it usually didn't take long for the newcomer to catch on.

What I received were jobs that clearly no one had needed to do previously.

Cleaning on top of the lockers was, frankly, disgusting. There was muck and dead insects and mold up there, which had obviously been left to grow for a while. The gap between the ceiling and the lockers was slim, and I managed to hit my head five times at least before I stopped trying to stretch my back out and just accepted the cramps around my lower spine.

By the time the alarm went off, I was grateful to do something that was actually part of my job. Jase jumping into the truck with Hawke, Zander, Gage and Carmen seemed almost too obvious. Given they were all bulky men and even though Carmen was a more slender body, there still would have been more room in the truck with Johnson, Mark, and me. But given that he had avoided me all morning and specifically left smaller rooms when I entered made it pretty clear he didn't want anything to do with me.

"I don't like conflict in the team, but I would suggest you avoid Jase," Johnson piped up as we drove. "He's got you pegged as an asshole, and the team is family, so you gotta prove yourself before they'll do anything except have his back."

"He's already said something?" I asked, a sinking feeling in my stomach.

"He said something to Mark, and Mark has decided to take it upon himself to see if you really are still as bad."

"Ah, I see." I sighed. "So I've got a world of hard work and patience-testing coming my way?"

"Pretty much. I can talk to them if you want?" Johnson offered.

Smiling slightly, I shook my head. "Thanks, but I'm all right. I know I'm not a good memory for Jase. I was hoping to be able to prove I've changed, so this might actually work for me." I laughed softly.

Johnson glanced my way while he paused at a red light. "You really are odd, but if you can look at it that way, you will probably be fine."

"Thanks for the heads up, though."

"Just don't want my job to become a warzone." He shrugged.

At the site of the fire, even though the

blaze had grown to take over the kitchen, I was instructed to stay outside and keep anyone from entering. It was a shitty task to be given and usually reserved for a Probee, not a seasoned firefighter. After all, civilians never really ran into a burning building—that only happened in rare cases and movies.

There was a little girl, however, who was crying loudly.

"Hey, kid," I crouched down in front of her and her mother. "It's okay. It'll all be done in a bit."

"B-but..." She whimpered.

"She's worried our cat is still inside," her mother explained.

I glanced at the girl with tears trailing down her cheeks and fear etched all over her face. "Hey, sweetie. Is your cat clever?"

Sniffing in the disgustingly loud way only a child can, she rubbed her nose on the sleeve of her shirt. "Uh-huh. He's super clever. He even knows how to get into my room when mom shuts my door at night."

A small chuckle left my lips at the childlike innocence in that piece of information. Worked in my favor, though. "So, if he's that clever. Do you really think he would still be inside? And if he is, don't you think he's found a safe place under a bed far away from the fire?" I raised an eyebrow with a small smile as I watched the little girl think about it.

"That's true..." she finally mumbled before nodding quickly.

"See. Clever kitties are usually just fine." I gave her a small wink before nodding to her mother, who mouthed a word of thanks at me.

"Oi, Sanders. Quit slacking off. We need an extra oil fire kit!" Jase yelled across to me from the door. Resisting the urge to roll my eyes at his words, I turned and jogged back to the truck I had arrived in and dug out the foam required to douse the fire inside. Once mixed with their powder hose, it would be just fine. Tossing it over to Jase, I watched him race back inside, not missing the irritating look on his face he had just from having to interact with me.

This was going to be a long road to getting Jase to understand I wasn't going to make his life hell just because I still existed.

The fire was easily brought back under control by the team. We hadn't really needed two trucks on sight, but with an oil fire, you could never be sure how it was going to turn out. Some members of the public knew how to deal with them, while others made it a million times worse in their panic.

"So, what caused the fire? And why did it take the authorities so long to arrive that it was able to spread?" A voice followed me up and down the perimeter that I was making sure stayed clear of civilians. I turned my gaze onto the female with blonde hair pulled back in a bun and a notepad in her hands.

Journalists.

God, I hated them.

I wouldn't mind them so much if they ever wanted to put a positive spin on everything, but these days the media tended to give more grief and cause more doubt and fear.

JASE

"Please, stay back. This is still a live fire scene," I replied without acknowledging any of the questions. It was people like her that meant tax money had to fund PR teams for something that should have been left at fighting fires and saving lives.

"People are saying you all took a long time to respond. Too busy playing on the pole?" She smirked, making me realize she wasn't even a news journalist. She likely had a conspiracy blog or worked for a tabloid that truly just fuelled chaos and mistrust.

"Any questions you have can be answered by the station," Carmen called to the woman as she stepped over to me and handed me a new hose head. "Run that inside, will you?" She raised an eyebrow, and I realized that she was saving me from the overly nosey woman.

Nodding my thanks, I took the chance to jog over to the house and head inside. There was less smoke damage than I expected, and I quickly found Johnson holding the hose, which had malfunctioned.

"Here's the new one!" I called, swiftly moving around to the front of him while he choked off the flow of foam so I could remove the old head and replace it with the new one.

"Where's Carmen?" he asked.

"Saving me from a journalist," I laughed honestly.

"Didn't fancy fifteen minutes of fame?"

"I just want to do my job. I don't need a tabloid painting me in any light." I shook my head and backed up so Johnson could get back to work. Through his visor, I could see him level me with a curious look before getting back to it.

Perhaps I would have some chance of proving myself. From then on I delved into anything else that needed doing to help the crew inside doing most of the fight.

"I thought you'd done this job before," Jase grumbled as we got out of the over layers of our uniform once back at the station.

"I have," I replied with a raised eyebrow, wondering what part of my day he had a problem with. Everything had gone well, there were no casualties, and the fire was out with only damage done to the kitchen itself.

"Then why the hell were you off flirting with some mother and child while there was a fire to be fought?" Mark stood with his arms folded, leaning against his locker with a judgmental eyebrow raised, waiting for the answer.

I took in a slow breath to keep my tone even and my aura patient. I couldn't let my annoyance at the way they thought I would fob off my job take this into an emotional argument that would only isolate me further.

"You told me to keep the public back," I started. "That little girl was scared because she thought her cat was still inside the building, and I wanted to ensure we weren't at risk of her running in to find the creature."

Later on, she had spotted the cat in the neighbor's front garden and immediately shot out from her mother's arms and climbed the fence to grab the little white kitten.

"I was doing the job that was given to

me with as much observation of the environment and situation as I could," I continued calmly. "If you would like me to act differently to meld with the team better, I would welcome the advice."

"You're such an arrogant sonofabitch," Jase grunted at me before stalking off, throwing his uniform at his locker without bothering to close it.

"But. I..." I glanced at Mark, who did nothing more than roll his eyes and wall away as well.

What was I supposed to have done?

Apologized and said I wouldn't do it again. That would have been bullshit as I knew in the exact same scenario, I would try to calm the child again to stop her from possibly harming herself.

Swallowing my frustration, I shook my head and tried to push it out of my mind.

Unfortunately, it wasn't the only time in the first couple of months that Jase took issue with how I acted when out on jobs.

"I'm doing the jobs I'm given! What is your problem?" I eventually snapped at him after another snide comment slipped from his lips. I knew where this had come from, and I knew I shouldn't bite and argue back, but I couldn't stand having my attitude toward my job questioned. This was a job I loved, a job I took originally as a way to level my cosmic karma, but I fell in love with the variation it could bring, the different people you could meet, and the energy of a team that worked together.

God, I missed my old team.

"You know exactly what my problem is," Jase spat back.

"Oh, get over yourself. You fucking

child," I growled angrily. How dare he be so petty as to take some bullying from childhood and turn it into actions that could potentially fuck with my career? "I'm good at what I do."

"You're an arrogant prick."

"Better than a sniveling coward who needs the rest of his team to give me the shitty jobs and crap attitudes so you can remain on the high ground," I snarled, pushing myself away from the truck I had been told to clean. Throwing the sponge with force onto the ground at Jase's feet, splattering him with dirty soapy water, I glared at him. I was officially done trying to prove I was a good person by just smiling politely. If he couldn't find it in him to have a simple conversation with me after two months of working together... Well, fuck him.

"Clean your own fucking truck," I spat out before storming out of the room and heading for the Captain's office. If Jase wanted me off the team so badly, he was getting his way. I wanted to be away from him and on another one as soon as humanly possible. I wasn't going to take *no* for an answer.

Captain Clarke was on a phone call when I arrived, which at least allowed me a little time waiting outside to calm down from the sheer frustration I had been feeling. At least, that was what I hoped the time would allow. Instead, I just found myself pacing up and down outside of the office door, getting more and more frustrated.

By the time I was welcomed inside, I was practically seething.

"How can I help you, Sanders?"

Captain Clarke asked as he motioned for me to take a seat across from him.

"I want to be transferred to another team," I said without hesitation, obviously attempting to keep my voice at a steady level.

Captain Clarke raised his eyebrow in my direction. "And why is that?"

I fell into an explanation of what had been happening over the last few months. The extra work, which wasn't exactly kosher, the criticism of my work, the past that Jase and I had, and how I felt he was discriminating against me because of it.

"I just want to be able to do my job," I continued, having calmed down a little from my rant.

The Captain sighed softly. "I have no spaces in the other teams to move you into. I know you are good at your job. The

EVE RILEY

fact you are is the main reason you even survived what happened in New Orleans. But I need you to mesh with this team, or I have nothing else to offer you here."

I growled softly in frustration.

"So what am I supposed to do?" I asked.

"I'll think of something." The Captain sighed before waving me out with his hand when his phone rang again.

Damn it.

So much for getting any solutions from him. Heading back to the central room, I punched some numbers into the vending machine to get some solid sweets to chew on as I went back to my uniforms that I had yet to clean.

Ignoring the dirty looks I got from Jase and the rest of the team, I spent the rest of the day scrubbing out burn marks and scuffs from my uniform and the truck Johnson drove. He hadn't been the most friendly per se, but he had also been the only one other than Carmen who also actually treated me like a colleague, and when I jumped onto his truck during callouts, I actually felt like I was doing my job rather than being some rookie that just got in the way.

A few hours later, the Captain came back in with his solution.

"Right, I've had enough of this whole tension and bickering within the team," he announced gruffly, looking around and settling his gaze for longer on everyone but Carmen. He obviously knew she was the only one here, not making anything worse.

Captain Clarke raised a hand as Jase opened his mouth to speak. "Don't start. I don't have any resources to change the teams around. Therefore, my only choice is to force you two to work together properly."

What did that mean?

"Quinn, you and Johnson will be swapping trucks. Jase, you and Quinn will work together on the two-man calls instead," he said.

"What?" Jase protested.

"Johnson?" The Captain turned to raise an eyebrow at him. "That okay with you."

"I'll work wherever, Captain." He nodded, glancing between Jase and me as though wondering if either of us would survive working with just the two of us. Somehow... I doubted it if the way Jase stormed out of the doors at the end of the day was anything to go by.

CHAPTER TEN

Jase

A PIERCING RINGING in my ears hammered at my skull. I couldn't be forced to work with Quinn.

How could Cap even think to insist on that?

Didn't I get any fucking say in the matter?

Anger bubbled in my chest, fueled me

as I hastily stomped to my car, slamming the door and throwing my head back, howling my frustration into the silence of the stifling, lung-burning air.

The sharp blade rested on the edge of the tub, its brushed metal finish glinting in the flickering lights from above the sink.

The water in the tub sloshed toward the edges as I slipped inside its over-heated depths, the temperature of the clear liquid turning the skin on my legs and abdomen crimson almost instantly. I reveled in the pain, tears tracking down my cheeks, the taste of salt forming on my lips, finally freed from the heat that had gathered behind my eyes since that moment in the courtyard only mere hours ago. I wouldn't let them see me cry then, I couldn't let them know how much they hurt me, but now I could let every single ounce of that torment free to reign, reminding me of the bitterness of humiliation, the sting of embarrassment on my skin, the sour taste of defeat as the world seemed to close in and choke off the breath from my lungs.

I wished for a moment that the pain of the scalding bathwater was enough, that it would give me some sort of relief from the internal crushing pain of the sentiment that I didn't belong, I was a 'waste of space', as Quinn had repeatedly told me so many times this year, but that respite was not granted. I had to assume I didn't deserve that kind of reprieve.

I sobbed, my breath hitching in my chest as I strained to hear anything outside the bathroom door. A creak of the floorboards, the phone ringing, the sound of a car in the driveway. Anything to tell me that I was no longer alone. Nothing came. Not even the chipper bark of a dog from the neighbor's yard or the trill of a bird playing its blissful notes broke through the oppressive silence surrounding me.

I was truly and utterly alone.

Steam covered the mirror, the gathered condensation marking jagged tracks down the reflective glass much in the way I would assume the tears spoiled the smoothness of my skin.

My heartbeat thudded behind my breastbone, the need to make it stop, to end the daily torment of my life a palpable living being that lodged itself inside my very soul. This was the only way to cease the suffering. I couldn't take it anymore.

The bite of silver-colored rectangle sliding effortlessly over the delicate soft skin of my wrist felt so much more *soothing than being slammed into unforgiving metal of the lockers at school. More pleasing than the inevitable tear of my teeth through my lips as I fought to hold on, not to respond or react to Quinn and his buddies' incessant torture and repeated assaults. Somehow, the razor slicing through my skin was easier, simpler to bear, and for a heartbeat or two I watched, a small smile gracing my lips, pleased as the scarlet blood welled up at the site of the neatly parted skin.*

As the scent of copper reached my nose, I marveled at the unique and diverse patterns each drop made in the water, swirling around, becoming heavier than the water from the tap, pausing in suspended animation for a moment, and then finally falling, melting through the glassy surface to coat the bottom of the tub beside my leg in dotted splendor.

As my pulse began to thrum slower, an electric kind of buzz taking up residence in my ears and spreading over my skin, the pressure in my chest eased and I sucked in a deep, shuddering breath.

With that single breath I suddenly felt so clean, so relieved, so free...

A stuttered sigh slipped from my lips as my head lolled to the side, the panic receding, all thoughts fleeing my mind and letting me sink into the numbness. All the torment ended, every single trickle of my humiliation ended as I watched the bathtub water turn a pretty brilliant ruby red.

Only two insignificant beats later, thunder rolled and the resonance of the community of dogs yipping, the unmistakable quick chirpy squeal of tires *on hot pavement, that creak of the wood enveloping footsteps in the hallway that I'd so longed to hear finally reached my fuzzy mind. The echo of my name slipping from my mother's lips reaching in and tugging, even as harsh movements reverberated in the bathwater as someone viscously banged their fists on the door.*

The crack of wood splintering filled the room with a roar as the door suddenly imploded and broken screaming reached through my muddled brain to stain my psyche much in the way my blood now covered and pigmented every inch of my pale, tattered skin.

I stared into the water, my eyes unseeing, the piercing pitch of a jacked up feminine tone making my ears hurt, pulling me from my newfound comfort and peace, the intrusion burrowing uninvited through my tranquility like an axe slicing through wood.

Letting my eyes fall shut, I gave into the darkness that now surrounded me, the voices fading like they might as if I'd reached the other end of a long tunnel.

Sweet blissful relief finally overtook me and I breathed out that last shred of excruciating tension.

CHAPTER ELEVEN

Jase

"I CAN'T BELIEVE he actually wants me to work with that bastard!" I exclaimed over a pint that evening down at the local steakhouse bar, which Johnson and I frequented every other week. It was a quaint place run by a mother and daughter pair who somehow kept the food top quality while keeping the atmosphere chilled. From inside, it was almost like it was a joint you'd found on the side of a highway or in a smaller town where everyone knew each other.

"You'll be fine, just do your job as you usually do, and it'll quickly show up how he gets in the way." Johnson chuckled, waving over the daughter with a small awkward grin. It was hilarious to watch him attempt to flirt with her and fail every time.

Ruth was a badass redhead who rocked tight leather trousers and crop tops. She kept her hair in a fishtail braid, and she was the queen of pool around these parts. So many had tried to win against her with her phone number as the winning prize, and she had wiped the floor with every single one. Johnson had it bad. Even though he was a masculine being, he became flustered whenever she came over.

"All right, boys. What can I get you?" she chimed, flashing a wink in our direction and smirking knowingly when Johnson stumbled over his order.

Rolling my eyes at him, I laughed softly. "Double cheeseburger with bacon."

"Thought firefighters were meant to be healthy?" She laughed.

"Well, it's been a shit day." I sighed. "We'll have a couple more rounds too."

"Damn. What happened?"

"Jase has his panties in a bunch over having to work with the new guy." Johnson chuckled.

I scowled at him both for making me sound childish but also pushing out the idea that I might be wearing panties. God, the image that went through my mind was enough to make me recoil.

Who the fuck would want a man in panties?

"I don't have my *panties* in a bunch," I growled.

"Fine. Your tighty whities then." Johnson rolled his eyes.

"I prefer the image of panties." Ruth laughed with a wink sent my way. Okay, apparently, Ruth wouldn't mind a man in panties. Johnson had clearly had the same thought as he spluttered around his beer while she walked away cackling.

"You've gotta know she's messing with you every time you come in, right?" I asked Johnson with a laugh.

"I know. She prefers older men too, so you're more her type anyway." Johnson sighed.

Glancing over at the bar Ruth had

ventured behind to fetch our drinks, I briefly wondered for the billionth time in my life how much easier it would be if I was attracted to women. I could have found someone like her who could give banter as well as she took it, who could drink with the men and laugh with the women. My parents would have been happy, and they wouldn't ask every other weekend when I was going to find myself a 'nice girl to settle down with'.

If only it was that simple. I was about as likely to do that as I was to get on well with Quinn at work.

The thought of the man annoyed me to no end. Especially because—and I would only ever admit this in my own head—he was everything that I found attractive. I had found myself in almost nightly naughty dreams with him as the centerpiece once or twice since he had turned up. They started out as memories of a sort, reminders of those times in school where he'd beaten me down both mentally and physically, until they changed and became the type of dreams I'd never have expected Quinn Sanders to star in.

Heated ones.

Ones that resulted in my waking with my boxers soaked in my own cum.

In them, he was still a bit of an asshole, but I loved it.

Fuck, I practically begged for it.

I hated those dreams. Working so close to him was not going to help me chase them away any.

I suspected it was because I had been thinking so much about him lately. But that night, he appeared in my dreams again.

I was at the station after a call. It had been a smoke-heavy callout, but no one had been hurt. I often tended to linger a little longer in the showers after a call like that as I had figured out that the cat that occasionally visited my house didn't like smokey scents, so in order not to chase off the creature, I had taken to lengthening my time in the showers.

The water was hot and comforting, pounding down on my shoulders, which were sore from work. I rubbed at the muscles slowly, letting out a small groan. My fingers weren't quite long enough to reach my shoulder blades properly, but they had a decent level of strength to press into the knots near my neck and I breathed a sigh as I finally began to loosen them.

"Need help with that?" His deep voice

was low and sultry. I didn't even have to look around to know it was Quinn.

"Piss off," I grumbled at him with half the effort I would use normally.

"You don't want that. Not really."

"Arrogant ass," I growled, though his strong hands on my shoulders, thumbs rubbing the aching flesh with a fragrant soap, made the growl quickly turn into a soft breathy moan.

"Arrogant, but very good with my fingers." Quinn chuckled in my ear as he pressed up behind me. This was always the way. I never really saw him in my dreams, he was always behind me, always in control, but I knew it was him. His height made it easy to curl over me slightly as his chest pressed to my back. I could feel the way his chest and arm muscles flexed as his hands continued to *massage my shoulders, then down my arms.*

I never fought back. Even if we were in the showers at work, somehow, that only enhanced my need. Leaning my head back against his shoulder, my eyes fell closed when his hands moved to massage my front.

"They are good fingers." I moaned softly. They were. I noticed them a lot when he was working with both heavy and delicate equipment. They were strong and agile, careful and precise. They were the kind of fingers I imagined could pick me to pieces easily.

I felt Quinn smirk against my ear, and soon his tongue was running along the edge of it. "You need to keep quiet, or someone might hear you," he whispered, his fingers and thumbs finding my nipples and giving them a teasing pinch.

I wanted to say I didn't care. I wanted to tell him that I wanted him to make me scream in pleasure and screw anyone who had a problem. But even in my dreams, I was terrified of anyone knowing what I was.

"I can't..." I whimpered pathetically.

"Don't worry, I'll help." Lifting his left hand to cover my mouth, he paused for a moment waiting for my nod of approval, before he trailed his right hand down my back between us.

I had not been with many men, but I knew I enjoyed being the bottom. It was something I usually felt ashamed of, but in my dreams, I was able to arch my back and press my ass into the hand that grabbed and squeezed at the cheeks with eagerness. Unable to speak, I nipped at the palm of Quinn's hand as an encouragement.

I heard nothing more than a chuckle as a warning before his hand left my ass, and I heard the click of a bottle. I hissed at the cool feeling of lotion or conditioner as his fingers ran over my tight hole. More gently than I imagined Quinn could ever truly be, he pushed one digit inside me and slowly shifted it against the walls of my insides, letting me get used to the feeling.

I wanted more. I was burning deep within for more. With his hand still over my mouth, the only way I could show him that desire was to push back on his hand.

"So needy..." he purred against my neck, not wasting any time by pushing another two fingers inside me. He pulled me back close against his chest as I

shuddered and writhed at the pleasure of his fingers brushing against the most sensitive glands bundled up there.

I was needy. And in my dreams, I was allowed to be needy.

Lifting my arms to reach behind my head, I slid my fingers into that short black spiky hair and curled them against his scalp, mumbling against his palm. When he pulled it away just slightly, I heard myself whine out a plea.

"Fuck me." God. I wanted it so badly. And from the feeling of hard heat against my hip, Quinn wanted it to.

"Say please," he whispered teasingly.

"Please!" The word came easily, and I found myself being shoved forward against the cold tiles of the shower room. Quinn's hand splayed out against the tiles to support himself as his other hand *withdrew from my body and held my hips in place.*

My mouth was dry with anticipation, and my body practically trembled with want.

Fuck.

The sound of my alarm brought me back to reality. Panting softly and glancing down at myself, I couldn't even begin to deny the evidence of my dream that was all over the inside of my boxers. I could see the wetness from the outside of the blue material.

"What the fuck am I, a goddamned teenager again?" I growled to myself as I got out of bed and peeled the boxers from my body, slinging them into the hamper. I needed to get laid. Perhaps it was time I went out of town for a long weekend and went somewhere no one knew me to let off some steam.

I'd done it a few times, not so far away that anyone got suspicious, but far enough that no one would recognize a firefighter from Baton Rouge. Usually, I drove over to Lafayette, where I could go to a club called Bolt, which was extremely relaxed and friendly for the queer community. They welcomed everyone from the extremely out to the quietly closeted.

I could barely remember the last time I had been. Probably not since Trevor had retired.

Glancing down at myself in the shower, already reacting to the memories of the last time, I decided I would definitely go on the next weekend when I didn't have plans.

That thought was only cemented

further when I was at work later that day, and I had told Quinn that he could wash the truck. Hearing laughter from outside, I glanced out the window to see that Quinn had obviously slipped and dropped the hose, spraying water all over himself while Carmen laughed so hard that she had actually begun to snort a little.

If I could have been annoyed that they were getting along okay despite Carmen having been told about my issues with the man, I would have. But, it was heavily distracting to see Quinn's white shirt plastered to his body by the water.

Shit.

It was everything I imagined in my dreams when he was pressed against my back. Every inch of him was toned and well formed, and I could see the golden color of his tan through the wet, now see-through shirt.

"Quit fucking around! We have a call!" I yelled down from the window before storming back inside, hoping my blazing cheeks would calm in the time it took Quinn to change. It wasn't an urgent call, more along the "cat stuck in a tree" level urgency where they didn't really need anything but the ladder height we could provide. Still, it was a job, and the two-man team was being sent for it.

"Sorry, Jase," Quinn said as he jogged back out of the locker room with a fresh set of clothes on.

"Forget it. Just do the job." I rolled my eyes, still unable to give the man an inch of trust.

"Sure." He sighed. "What is the job?"

"Helping a couple down from a third floor as their stairs collapsed in," I replied, motioning for Quinn to get his ass in the truck so I could start the journey across town.

"Look, I get you aren't happy about being paired with me, but we can still do the job without needing to bitch at each other. All right?"

"Still calling people female terms to make them feel smaller?" I turned a glare at him briefly before looking back at the road.

"What?" Quinn sounded genuinely surprised. "No. I'm not misogynistic."

"Oh okay, just against feminine men... sure." We pulled up to the site, and I jumped out of the truck before Quinn could say another word.

I knew I was taking my frustration out on him even more so than I normally did, but every time he spoke, I heard the whisper in my ear from the night before, and at the same time, I also heard the younger version of Quinn calling me a girl because the hairstyle I had was longer and resembled one that was sported by a favored video game character back then.

By the end of the day, after snipping at Quinn after every single thing he did and listening to him growl in annoyance while biting back his own responses, I decided that I was just going to go to Lafayette at the end of this working period. I just couldn't wait any longer and I felt like I was about to explode.

"So, you aren't coming over for tea then?" My mother asked when I phoned her later that evening to let her know I wouldn't be by to visit this evening as previously planned.

"Sorry, Ma. Don't get many days that

Annie and my schedules work out so we can hang out," I explained, using my usual lie. Annie was a nickname for one of the drag singers at the club I wanted to go to, but it was also the name of a girl who used to live down the street who I got on with very well.

I was pretty sure my mother was under the impression that Annie and I had something going on, but we just never saw each other enough to make it work.

"I know, sweetie. I'll just miss you, is all," she sighed, her exaggerated disappointment making itself evident down the phone line as intended.

"Same. But I'll be there next time!" I reassured her with a smile on my face that I knew she couldn't see.

"Well, you better say hi to Annie from

me and get me the latest gossip from her life."

I laughed loudly. "I always do, mom." Even if it was always made up. "I'll also bring some of that pie back that you really like and drop it off on my way back into town."

"Oh! The apple and cinnamon?"

"Either that or the blueberry, your choice."

"Definitely the apple and cinnamon." My mother chimed happily. "You're such a gem!"

After a little more talk about how her week had been and me attempting not to rant too much about Quinn, in case she realized I was talking about the old preacher's son, I hung up the phone with a soft sigh. I hated lying to my mother, but I just couldn't see her ever smiling at the idea of me bringing a man home instead of a woman. And the idea of losing my family seemed too high a risk just for the so-called romance of love.

Still, at least I now had a few days to look forward to. Jumping onto my laptop, I picked through a couple of hotel websites I had come to know over the years. Ones whose staff looked the other way if someone came back with you and who didn't comment when you asked for the name on your room to be altered to one that didn't match your ID. The ones that understood that being gay in the deep south of the USA wasn't always the easiest or the safest thing even in the modern day and were happy to help in any way they could.

I specifically liked one known as the Phoenix Inn. It was more of a B&B, but you didn't get woken up for the breakfasts if you said upon arrival that you would be having a late night. It was run by two men who claimed to be business partners, and both said they had wives who had died not long ago. Personally, I suspected that was a front, and the main reason they were so discrete was due to the fact that they had spent their whole lives doing just that.

Unfortunately, they were all booked up, so I ended up booking the run-down motel that obviously didn't care who came in and out so long as they paid. It wasn't the most secure, and usually, I took some portable locks to add to the inside while I was there as a precaution, but it was located close to the club, and it was cheap, so it would do.

Getting through the next few days of

work was the hardest thing to do. Working with Quinn was annoying and frustrating and always left me both angry and in need of a cold shower. His ass just looked way too good in uniform. By the end of the week, I couldn't tell if I was angrier at him for being who he was, or at myself for finding him so ridiculously attractive. I had never fantasized about a specific person that wasn't some kind of airbrushed Adonis of a celebrity, and yet here I was doing just that over my bully from high school.

Just because he had grown up to be just my type, it didn't change that he was some homophobic piece of shit who would only torture me again if he ever found out I was really gay like he claimed all those years ago. Once the frustration was out of my system, I would be fine.

At least, that was the story I told myself all the way to Lafayette, with some classic 80's rock blasting from my pickup's radio. It was a pleasant drive, but I was antsy. I wanted to get there and find someone... anyone... to get me to stop thinking about Quinn.

CHAPTER TWELVE

Quinn

MY PATIENCE AND tolerance were wearing thin. Working so close with Jase and receiving the full brunt of his attitude was slowly but surely grating on all my nerves, and it was only a matter of time before my temper really snapped.

For fuck's sake, was the man really planning on holding a grudge from school for so long that he made the station a miserable experience for us all working there?

I knew that Johnson and Mark had Jase's back, but I refused to believe they wouldn't rather have a team that didn't cause tension so thick that you couldn't even cut it with a knife while waiting for callouts.

"You need to get out," Jared said over dinner at the end of my working week. "You've got three days off now, why not make the most of it? Go out, get laid." Jared chuckled.

It wasn't the worst idea in the world, but I couldn't stop myself from pulling an unconvinced expression. "I dunno..."

Jared raised an eyebrow and waited for me to elaborate.

"I'm not sure how comfortable I am

going out and trying to find someone to have sex with here... you know, in Baton Rouge, where I associate more people with religion."

"I suppose that makes sense. You haven't been back here all that long either," Jared mused. "You could take a couple of days in New Orleans."

"No," I replied too quickly. I hadn't told anyone why I had moved back to my hometown, but the memories that New Orleans held were still much too painful to consider returning.

What if I bumped into someone I had known, and they started to ask questions or make comments about the events back then?

That would definitely kill any buzz I might have managed to build up.

"Okay." Jared sighed. You could see

what Lafayette has to offer, though it's a smaller town than here.

I remembered going to Lafayette on a school trip, but I could barely remember a thing about the town itself. Pulling out my phone, I decided to have a quick look on Google to see if there were any decent clubs for my needs. Normal clubs were fine, but I wasn't ignorant to the fact that my tall, dark, tanned look often caught the eye of women rather than men if I didn't place myself somewhere that made people think I was gay. After all, the likelihood of a good-looking guy being gay when found at a gay club was considerably higher than at a regular club.

"Well, there's one place with pretty good reviews," I confirmed as I clicked on the website link from the maps.

JASE

"One place is all you need," Jared stated, placing a couple of fresh beers on the coffee table and flopping himself back into the chair. I hadn't even realized he had left the room.

"You wanna come?" I asked.

"As much as I love a drag show and cheesy music, I don't need to be around while you get laid, kiddo." Jared barked out a laugh and shook his head.

"I'm not a kid."

"Always will be to me."

I rolled my eyes at him before calculating the route. "It's not that far... I could go tonight and use tomorrow to chill." It was only about an hour's drive, and it had been a long time since I got to drive on an open road with my music playing.

It didn't take long to pack a few

clothes, toiletries, and bedroom necessities once I decided to go. I knew I wouldn't need too much, and I had some excess money, so I could afford a couple of lunches out or a hotel dinner if that was easier.

I hadn't booked anything yet, but it was midweek, and I suspected I would be able to walk into most places and be able to find a room.

Settling into my BMW was the easiest thing in the world. I knew it was an expense I didn't really need when living in a city, but for me to drive out of the city, my beautiful car was a blessing. Smooth drive, comfortable and supportive seats, and a damn good sound system.

Singing along to some 80's classic rock was always a successful way to make me relax. By the time I reached Lafayette, my mood was much lighter than it had been in days.

As I was not too fussy about where I stayed, I simply decided to pull into whatever parking lots I came across and ventured into the closest hotel until I found one with an available room.

It was nearly midnight when I actually arrived at the hotel, so there was little point in going out that night. I decided to grab a quick shower and then get some sleep. It was always nice just to freshen up a little after a hot car journey.

I could explore the town a little in the morning so I knew my way around before going out to intoxicate myself and find someone to let loose with. It would be a lot easier to deal with a drunken night if I knew where I was on my way out of the club. Especially considering how bad my sense of direction was after a couple of drinks.

It was a cheap hotel chain about a ten-minute walk from the center of the town. It was not flashy, but the bed linens were clean, and that was all I needed. The room had two beds with a desk in between them, two lamps on the walls, a closet, and an attached bathroom. It looked like it hadn't been updated since the 1970s, but for one night, I didn't care.

I glanced into the bathroom and found I did care a little about the fact the shower looked just as old. As long as the water was warm, at least, coming out of those metal bars. It smelled like bleach and there were no fancy showerheads or anything else to make it look nice but at least it was clean.

I turned on the water, allowing the

temperature to heat as I shucked off the clothes I'd worn to travel. Sliding under the hot spray, I sighed as I did a quick dash of shampoo over my hair, letting the hot water sluice over my skin for a minute, then rinsed my locks and grabbed the bar of hotel soap, lathering my body and making a half-assed effort to clean all the necessary crevices.

One hand braced against the slick wall, I closed my eyes as I wrapped my other hand around my sensitive head, spreading some of the soap along my engorged shaft. I moved down my length, gripping my cock in my fist, pulling and tugging slowly, building a rhythm. Faceless images flitted through my mind. Blond-brown hair, brilliant blue eyes, slick, tanned skin with freckles haphazardly speckled over the shoulders.

Then suddenly, the image changed.

Jase blushing before me on his knees, my fingers threaded through his hair as he looked up at me from under his lashes, his cheeks hollowed while he sucked me off, pushed to the forefront of my mind, and I groaned with pleasure at the thought.

Immediately, my cock twitched at the vision. I tugged harder, faster, as I imagined my cock hitting the back of his throat, his eyes widening and watering as he struggled to swallow my hardness. The sound of choking prevailing as I gripped his hair, my fists tightening in the strands, pulling him to me hard, burying myself in his warm heat.

My hips moved faster as my breathing intensified, and I thrust my cock desperately against my slick palm as I chased my orgasm through the clouds and haze of my imagination.

I pumped my cock, feeling the orgasm build to bursting nearly instantly and thick ropes of warm cum sprayed onto the wall of the shower as I reveled in the rush of sweet release, some sliding down over my hand as I fought to control the trajectory of my release and catch my breath.

I opened my eyes and stared at the ceiling with a mixture of remorse, regret, and desire that left me both sated and hungrier than I'd ever been before.

I turned off the water, feeling like an ass for even having thoughts like that of Jase.

Where the hell had they come from anyway?

Stepping out, I grabbed a clean white

towel from a stack above the toilet and dried myself off, dropping the towel on the counter as I flicked off the light and left the bathroom.

I pulled back the sheets of the bed closest to the bathroom and slid down onto the old-looking but surprisingly comfortable mattress, nodding off within minutes.

CHAPTER THIRTEEN

Quinn

WAKING FROM THE most decent night's sleep I'd had in weeks, I yawned and stretched, rolling out of the bed to hit the bathroom. I took a piss and brushed my teeth, then threw on the comfy clothes I'd packed in my duffel bag and grabbing the keycard, a light jacket, and my phone, I headed out into the bright sunshine.

Thankfully, while I wandered the streets, I discovered the town was fairly simple, and I noted that most of the roads would eventually lead me back in a circle to the central area where I was staying.

As the streets had not taken very long to work out, I decided that I could browse the shops and perhaps even catch a movie as a way to truly relax on a day off. Plus, if I happened to find a clothing shop or two I liked, there was no harm in having something new to wear tonight.

The day was a beautiful one. It was sunny but cool enough for me to want to keep my jacket on with the zip down. As it turned out, I didn't really need it for long. A little before lunchtime, I found myself overheating in the sunshine and having to carry the jacket over my arm.

I wandered through a few of the

shopping areas nearby, looking at different stores and trying to imagine what I would buy if money were no object. There was so much I wanted but couldn't justify buying. I really needed some new shoes or boots. My old pair had seen better days, and I had been wearing them practically every day since moving to Baton Rouge. They were well worn now, and I realized that they probably wouldn't last another month without needing to be replaced.

Eventually, I located a quirky little charity shop that actually had some decent clothes on offer. I browsed around a bit and picked up a couple of things; a nice pair of jeans, a casual shirt, and a soft leather jacket which looked like it might have been pricey originally but had obviously been donated by someone who had too many jackets or just got bored with it. Along with the clothing, I actually found a decent pair of boots in a box of heavily discounted shoes. I actually felt like I had done pretty well and gave myself a mental pat on the back for it.

I trekked my way back to a movie theatre I'd passed in my wandering earlier, happy to note they were playing a matinee of an older Tom Cruise movie followed by one with Richard Gere.

Who could resist an afternoon of watching sexy-as-sin hot man bod on the big screen, right?

I paid my entry fee, snagged a big bucket of popcorn with double butter, some M&Ms, and a super sized drink before settling into a seat in the back row in the near empty theater for an afternoon of action, intrigue, and romance. This was

JASE

definitely a great way to relax on a day off.

CHAPTER FOURTEEN

Quinn

DESPITE FINISHING THE entire bucket of popcorn and a bag of crunchy chocolate goodness during the movies, when I emerged from the theatre squinting at the bright light a few hours later, my stomach made itself known with a loud growl.

Before heading back to my hotel, I decided to stop at a small diner for food. It was reasonably busy for an early evening but not so busy that I couldn't hear myself think. Choosing a seat at the counter, I glanced over the menu. The diner was simple, but the details that were found in the decor and the presentation of the dishes that I could see suggested that there was great pride in the work here.

"Hi there, doll. What can I get for ya," the girl behind the counter chimed as she walked over to me. She was a beautiful brunette with a slightly wonky nose, cute little freckles, and green eyes that I had to admit matched mine in brightness. Her hair was cut short, which suited her and made her look more mature than the other kids her age. She wore a pair of jeans and a plain white T-shirt under the apron that was clearly the only uniform, but she looked like an expensive model rather than someone who lived in a small town like this and worked in a diner.

Usually, I'm more than happy to flash a charming smile at women to get them to settle into a conversation and provide information when I need it. But I had a feeling that I wouldn't need to do that with this woman. She seemed more than friendly already.

"What do you recommend?" I asked, flashing her a smile. "I'm Quinn, by the way. Nice to meet you."

"Katie." She smiled in return. "Are you here for a meal or just a snack?"

"Meal. I'm going out tonight, so something heavy enough to keep me going for the night, but not put me into a food coma, " I mused, glancing over the choices.

"Oh, a night out. I miss those." She chuckled softly. "I'd go with the classic burger with a helping of our paprika chips. That way there's a lot of carbs to keep up with an exciting night but yet not overkill, if you know what I mean."

"I'll have that then," I decided. "And a coffee if you have vanilla syrups."

"A man with a sweet tooth. I'll have to tell my fiancé he's not the only one who likes coffee syrups."

"Oh, definitely not. I've always been partial to sweet drinks. Not so keen on a lot of deserts, though," I admitted. I had always been an appetizer and main course kind of person rather than a main and desert.

"Ah, not quite so alike." Katie chuckled, beginning to brew a new pot of coffee. "If it's a sweet snack, he'll finish it in seconds."

"My father was like that." I laughed, finding it nice to just relax and talk to someone new without having to think or worry about what they were going to say next. "Do you have to hide snacks just to make sure you still have some waiting at a later date?"

"That's a good idea. But we don't live together yet."

"Oh?" I had to admit, that surprised me. She spoke like they were so close that it made sense for them to live together.

"We want to. But we both study, so it's hard to get enough money saved up," Katie explained.

"Understandable. What are you studying?" I asked, finding myself getting lost in the conversation rather than waiting impatiently for my meal.

"I'm studying to be a nurse. He's aiming to become an astrophysicist."

"And you both work as well? Damn."

"I know. We barely see each other." She laughed as though reading my mind. "But we have our goals, and when we have enough money, we'll buy a place, and we can see each other whenever we are home." She almost sounded dreamy as she spoke. There was a familiar stab of envy in my chest as my smile softened while watching her eyes sparkle as she spoke of their plans.

I would truly love to find such a connection one day. To find someone who had my back while I had theirs, even if I couldn't be home at all the same times as them. It had taken me a long time to accept that it was okay to want that kind of future. After growing up believing that being gay was wrong, I never really thought I'd ever be allowed to find a love like that. But now, after finally living life a little in New Orleans and coming into the man I really wanted to be, I think it's more than worth trying for. Now that I'd finally accepted myself the way I am, that the past was the past and the only thing I could do now was make the future better—with no more regrets, guilty feelings, or second thoughts about what I deserved—maybe the right person was just waiting out there somewhere, ready to catch me when I fell.

Though I doubted I'd find the love of my life in a club in a town that wasn't even where I lived. Oh well, I supposed I hadn't come here for love, after all. I had come here solely to let out some frustration.

I could find love another time.

The meal was as fantastic as advertised, and I had to admit I probably ate more than I should have before a night out. My stomach poked out just slightly, but I hoped that by the time I was dressed, at the club, dancing, and had caught someone's attention, it would have shrunk back to my usual toned look with tempting hips.

Looking at myself in the mirror as I pulled on a black shirt that was tight enough to show off my arms, but not too tight, I smirked softly. I knew I was hot. I wasn't about to deny it. The dark jeans I wore curved around and highlighted my backside, and even though I wasn't usually a bottom in the bedroom, I did delight at it being grabbed in encouragement. I had to admit, I found it fun when a guy would stare at me like he'd never seen anything so delicious before. It didn't happen often, but every now and then there were those guys who couldn't take their eyes off of me.

The thought made my smirk grow and I turned away from the mirror. Okay, I was definitely more than ready for a night of fun.

CHAPTER FIFTEEN

Quinn

THE CLUB, IT turned out, may have been the only one in town, but it was kitted out for everything a guy might need. There were a few rooms, and one was quieter on the music front, so a conversation could actually occur without having to go and stand outside. I thought that was one hell of a good touch. The number of times I had had to go and stand in a smoking area just to have a conversation with someone, even though they didn't smoke either, was insane. Here I would be able to buy them a drink, stand comfortably in the warmth, and focus on them rather than the fog of smoke surrounding me.

The drinks on the menu were all named strangely, not one of them giving away what they would actually taste like until you read the small print of ingredients underneath. With a chuckle at the name *Buttery Nipple*, I ordered two of those plus a simple rum and coke. I would normally go for vodka mixes, but the buttery nipple contained a cream-based liqueur, so vodka would have been a bad mix.

"God, that's good," I said to myself after the shots were gone, and I was able to bask in the aftertaste.

Walking through the club, I glanced around, taking in just how many people were there, even on a weekday. There appeared to be some kind of drag show mixed with karaoke that night. There were already a few people putting their names down on the list along with what they wanted to sing.

I kept walking, checking out everyone and everything as I went. Some folks were clearly here for the drinks while others looked like they were here for whatever was going on upstairs. A couple of guys had others hanging off them, obviously on dates or at least trying to look like they were on dates. They didn't have much luck though, since every time one of them would look back over his shoulder, I'd see their partner giving me an evil eye. It wasn't hard to figure out why either. It seemed like most of the men in the place were looking at me.

I smiled widely and waved at several groups who gave me a friendly wave back but no more than that. One guy even tried to get my attention by singing off key and horribly at the top of his lungs. Oh, I did love a gay bar. It was the only place that I could truly enjoy men checking me out rather than women.

"Hey there, handsome."

I glanced around at the voice and found a beautiful blond guy smiling at me. He was young, probably in university for some kind of sports, if his body was anything to go by.

"Hi." I smiled lightly.

"You here alone?" he asked. "Want to come and dance with us?" He motioned to a small group of friends who were already on the dance floor.

I didn't even offer any subtlety as I dragged my gaze down from his face to his body. He was dressed in fashion brands he probably couldn't afford without student loans, but he looked good.

"All right." Draining my drink and placing the glass on a side table, I followed him out on the dance floor.

It became clear pretty quickly; however, it wasn't him who had been interested in me. Soon enough, he and all his friends had edged away slightly, leaving a small brunette with a shaggy fringe. I wasn't even convinced he was of drinking age, and as he smiled up at me and danced closer, I felt an ominous concern in my gut.

I felt like a predator.

The moment I got the chance, I smiled gently at the brunette and made a motion with my hand that I was going to go for a drink. I picked the timing for the center of a song he seemed to be really enjoying, and thankfully, he didn't seem too interested in following me. I felt a little bad for deceiving the kid, but I would have been plain and honest with him if he had followed. Not my scene.

The bar had increased its number of patrons queuing for drinks by the time I returned, and it took a while to get to the front. Taking three more shots of the same kind and ordering another rum and coke, I moved to step back and felt my heel press down on another's foot as my arm bumped into them.

"Oh, I'm sorry!" I called over the music, turning my head to face them and hoping they weren't going to take an unnecessary level of offense. The face I found there was one I recognized so very clearly. Gorgeous soft brown eyes, the gentle slope of the jaw, messy brown hair obviously styled more carefully for a night out.

"Jase?"

I had to be dreaming, right?

What in the hell would Jase be here for?

He was straight, wasn't he?

I had heard him talking to Johnson and Mark about women and laughing about times back in college.

Right now, Jase was looking at me with the most terrified expression I had ever seen on anyone. I could see the cogs in his mind freeze up and panic take over as he tried to turn and leave without acknowledging me.

Reaching out, I grabbed his arm to stop him from leaving. I'm not sure why I did, but the idea of him being here was mind-boggling, and I needed to ask.

"Jase... are you bi?" I asked slowly. Perhaps he was curious about men but not sure how to go about it, so he wanted to test it out in a city he wouldn't bump into someone he knew.

Oh, the irony isn't lost on me if that was the case.

"What? No!" Jase snapped.

I raised an eyebrow at the defensiveness in his voice. Okay. He was definitely still in the closet then, whatever his sexuality.

"What about you? Come to torment some more gays?" Jase prickled.

"No. I am gay."

Jase seemed flabbergasted by the

news.

"What?"

"I'm gay," I repeated. "A cumgobbler. Queerboy."

"But the shit you used to give me..."

I could definitely see why he would be so confused after how I was when I was younger, but I had never hidden it since coming back to Baton Rouge. I was sure I had made more than one comment about how I wasn't interested in women when the guys had accused me of flirting. But apparently, none of that had overwritten Jase's memories of me, and I realized that Jase would need more of an explanation here. Sighing softly, I dropped my hand to take hold of Jase's, leading him to one of the quieter rooms.

Convincing Jase to sit down at a table, I brought over two beers and slid into the seat on the other side of the table.

"Jase, I need to apologize to you. I should never have done the things I did and said back in school," I started. "I already knew I was gay. I even had a crush on a guy a year above me. I was terrified, and I was angry. Everything I used to call you, tease you about, that was me hiding my truth from myself and everyone else. My parents and our community had raised me to believe that what I felt and who I was, was wrong. It was a sin to like another boy, and so I hid it the best way I knew how... which, looking back, was a really stupid way." It was strange saying all of this without Jase even responding from across the table. He just watched me, his brown eyes wide and questioning as he took a couple of large gulps from his drink.

"I thought if I was big and tough and handsome and good at sports and spoke about God enough, I could point at other people and deflect any suspicion of sin away from me," I continued. "I hate myself for that. I really do."

Jase surveyed me with eyes full of scrutiny, looking for any kind of lie he could find. But he wouldn't be able to. Every word was the absolute truth.

"I came out to my parents when I was living in New Orleans. Yet, they *still* try to set me up with girls every time I speak to them." I rolled my eyes and let out a tired chuckle.

"Was it hard?" Jase finally asked. "Coming out to them," he clarified as I looked up from my beer.

"One of the hardest things I've ever had to do," I admitted. "But I had some supportive friends in New Orleans who helped me through the six months where I wasn't sure if dad would ever accept it. I drank so much." I laughed, reflecting on the descriptive first few years of college. "At least I got it out of my system then, though."

Jase let out a sigh. "Well... I'm not straight, but no one knows."

Not straight.

That could mean anything, but the way Jase shifted in his seat, he was clearly uncomfortable with just admitting that vague statement. So I decided not to pry; instead, I nodded with a slight smile.

"I'm so very sorry for everything I did at school. That probably hasn't helped."

"It really didn't." Jase half-laughed, flashing me a shy smile, almost as though he couldn't believe he was having this conversation.

CHAPTER SIXTEEN

Jase

I COULDN'T BELIEVE that Quinn was gay. It explained so much... Actually, it kind of explained everything.

He also seemed to genuinely regret the way he was back at school.

I wasn't sure I was ready to forgive what he had done and the damage he had added to an already fairly intolerant school, but I felt something inside me change that night.

Perhaps it was the slightest bit of respect?

I couldn't deny the strength it must have taken Quinn to come out to his deeply religious parents. It was the courage I had never been able to find, and my parents didn't even tell me regularly that being gay or different was a sin.

"So, how come you decided to come to Lafayette rather than just go out in Baton Rouge?" I asked after a couple of moments.

Quinn slowly let out a breath and shrugged his shoulders. "I know I'm out as gay, but I still feel uncomfortable flaunting it in the same town as my parents."

Thinking over that, I couldn't say I

blamed him for that. Going out and being seen with another man would only cause more tension in his family.

"It'd be worth it if I was dating them, but just for one night of fun, it doesn't seem worth it." Quinn chuckled. "So, what about you? I assume you are here because it's easier to keep not being straight a secret if you don't go out where you might already know people?"

I nodded slowly.

"Don't worry. I won't tell anyone," Quinn reassured me with a smile that was soft and believable, even if I really didn't want to believe the man who had bullied me so badly back then. But, I supposed there was nothing I could do now apart from trust him. Quinn knew the truth, and I couldn't change that fact. Either he would tell, or he wouldn't.

"I'll get us some more drinks," Quinn finally said, probably realizing I was stuck on the same train of thought, unable to find a way to the end of it. "Would you like some shots? I've been having the buttery nipples."

I laughed quickly, having not expected such a phrase to leave his lips. "Buttery nipples?" I asked incredulously. "I think I'll stick with Jaeger."

Quinn laughed lightly and shook his head. "Sure, because that isn't just a cough syrup knockoff. You have absolutely no leg to stand on when judging me."

I soon discovered that just sitting, chatting, and drinking with Quinn was actually rather fun. He was quick-witted and sarcastic, which I already knew, but when it was paired with a man who was smiling, and it wasn't in response to something spiteful either myself or the others had said, it was a fun combination, and I found myself laughing a lot. Ironically, I was actually enjoying myself and I felt like a weight had been lifted off my shoulders.

"You've actually had the 'save a cat from a tree' callout?" I laughed after hearing one of the most stereotypical fireman stories in the books.

"Twice. The second time was because the old lady wanted tea with my colleague." Quinn laughed brightly. "He reminded her of her late husband, so he felt bad and agreed to have tea while I hung out with the cat we'd saved the previous week."

"You hung out with a cat?"

"Hey, don't knock it. Cats are cool

company."

"True. I have a stray one who visits my place almost daily now." I flashed him a smile. "She's a cute little grey thing, tiny as though she's not grown properly."

"Oh, poor thing."

"Yeah, I had her checked. She's not micro-chipped, so I figure I'll put food out for her and give her a worming treatment. Least I can do."

"That's good of you. Most would have just shooed her away or taken her to an animal shelter."

I shook my head quickly. "I thought about it, but they are such small cages, and she is used to being outside." I drained the last of my beer before adding. "Besides, sometimes she'll come and sleep on my bed if I leave the window ajar, which is very nice."

"Company in bed usually is." Quinn laughed.

I immediately raised an eyebrow, and smirked.

"That why you are here?" I didn't think a man as masculine as Quinn could blush, but his green eyes blinked twice as the color rose on his cheeks, and he glanced away.

"Maybe," he grumbled, bringing a half-mocking laugh from my lips. This time it was obvious that my teasing was not in a cruel sense.

"Well, what are you doing spending the whole night with me? Unless you think I'd bend over for you." I flashed him a flirty grin, slowly, vaguely realizing what I had said just a minute too late. Clearly the alcohol had gone to my head a little much if I was daring to flirt with someone I worked with. Never mind the fact that he had been my high school bully. Even if I was finding myself not despising him quite so much anymore.

I watched as a mixture of emotions ran over Quinn's face, but somehow I hadn't expected the mix to include lust.

"You shouldn't say things like that," Quinn started. "I tend to imagine ideas when they are put in my head like that."

I arched a brow and the words flew out of my mouth before I could stop them. "Oh really? And is that image a good one?"

"A very good one, so I would suggest you change the subject unless you are actually looking to rile me up." Quinn sent a challenging look my way.

It was tempting to keep going, though I couldn't say why. Perhaps it was the alcohol and the resulting lowered inhibitions. Perhaps it was simply because he was the most attractive man I had ever met, or perhaps it was because of the dreams I had been having over and over. Thankfully, I had the sense to know I would regret pushing those boundaries once I sobered up, and self-preservation finally kicked in. I raised my hands in defeat.

"All right, I'll stop," I agreed. "But considering we are both here to find someone for the night, we should probably be talking to more people than just each other."

"I suppose. But you are a good conversationalist." Quinn flashed me a smile and a wink.

"Turn that charm on for someone else. Come on, we'll find some people on the dance floor." I shook my head, pushing myself up from my seat and motioning for him to follow. I didn't much like dancing alone, but I would happily dance with someone and socialize with the people I found around us.

It was easy when people seemed to gravitate toward Quinn. He was taller than most of the men here, and even in the dark clothing he had chosen for the night, his muscles and rhythm were obvious.

I found a burning acidic feeling bubbling up in my gut as a youthful redhead with cute freckles danced up closer to Quinn, gaining his attention more than anyone else had done so far. I shouldn't have been jealous of that, I had no claim on the man, but shockingly, I did.

JASE

He didn't seem too interested in anything beyond the guy's body, though. The way he moved and swayed, the way he ran his hands up and down his arm while they both danced... It made me want to take Quinn by the hand and lead him away from all this madness.

But that was crazy right?

He was a colleague. He was my old bully and I was supposed to dislike him. He could dance and flirt with whomever he wanted. I had no right to be jealous. None.

So, why did the idea of him pressed up against anyone but me fill me with a bizarre anger that I could barely contain?

I wasn't sure why I reached out a hand to wrap around Quinn's wrist. The way the dark-haired male turned to look at me suggested he was just as confused.

"Jase..." he started, but I didn't want to hear it. Instead, I glanced once at the indignant-looking redhead before pulling Quinn forward and crashing my lips against his.

Part of my own mind screamed at my actions.

What the hell was I doing?

Kissing a man in public.

Kissing Quinn in public.

Second-guessing what I was doing, I moved to pull away when his arm looped around my waist and pulled me closer. Quinn kissed me with a passion I could never have dreamed up. I went weak in the knees, moaning into the kiss as his tongue pushed into my mouth and explored.

"I told you not to tempt me," he growled against my lips as he pulled back just slightly.

"Better than them tempting you," I grumbled. Before I could think about what I was doing, I let myself act on what my body wanted. "Come back to my place?"

Quinn raised an eyebrow, his eyes filled with questioning concern. "Are you sure?"

I hesitated for a moment, all the mocking and fears rolling around in my mind. I could back out now. Or I could actually have a connection with someone I knew, who knew me and who wouldn't look at me differently afterward.

"I'm sure." I nodded, beginning to step back toward the edge of the dance floor. "So, how about it?"

Quinn's eyes instantly darkened with a desire that lit my body on fire.

Fuck.

No one had ever looked at me that way.

"Let's go." I grabbed his hand and tugged him toward the door.

CHAPTER SEVENTEEN

Jase

IT DID NOT take long for us to get to the hotel I had booked myself into. Quinn chuckled a little at the awful 80s decor that made up the hallway, and once I pushed open the door, he smirked widely.

"You were hoping to get lucky in a room like this?" He chuckled, turning to me as my expression fell.

Was he about to leave me here?

"It's a damn good thing you are gorgeous enough that the room doesn't matter."

With that, he crowded me against the closed door and kissed me as though he was a starving man and I was the only meal in a million miles. My breath caught in my chest when he finally released my lips. He placed his forehead against mine before whispering, "I want you so badly."

"Quinn," I said on a soft sigh, not wanting to break the spell. He nipped my bottom lip, sending a bolt of desire straight to my core. His hand slid down my back until it wrapped around my ass and pulled me even more tightly against him.

"Do you want to be on the bottom or the top?" he mumbled against my lips.

JASE

Top.

I should have immediately said I wanted to be on top.

I moaned deeply as his leg pressed between my thighs, and his thick thigh rubbed against my already throbbing and engorged dick.

"Bottom," I panted out, surprising even myself.

"Really?" Quinn asked, astonishment lacing his voice.

I nodded eagerly. "Yes. I just... just... need..." God, I didn't know what I needed. Quinn seemed to think that there was something he understood in those words though, as he nodded and pressed himself tighter against my body, catching my lips with his once more.

Running my hands up his chest, I began to unbutton the shirt I had wanted to get under all night. His body was as gorgeous as I had expected, but I didn't get much of a chance to admire before he pulled me back toward the bed, turning until he was able to guide me until I fell onto the soft mattress. As I lay there, my breaths coming quickly, I watched as Quinn towered over me, slowly pulling his shirt off.

"It should be illegal to look that good," I mumbled, licking my lips.

Quinn laughed. "Well, thank you. I think I prefer the sight in front of me." He smirked, making me feel almost self-conscious, like a meal spread out for him. Self-conscious but powerfully aroused.

"Well, I'm not here for you just to stare at me." I lifted a hand to beckon him forward, something he did more than willingly. "Take off your pants," I ordered.

JASE

Watching Quinn do as I told him was thrilling, and even though it left me fully clothed with him crawling up the bed in just his boxers, I felt alive. His lips met mine once more, and he ground his hips down skillfully against mine. I could feel his size and length through his boxers and groaned into the kiss as his movements provided enough friction to rub my jeans against my own cock. He was just heavy enough to make me feel pinned but light enough that I could thrust my hips upward for more friction and know he would struggle to stop me.

If there was going to be a physical power play, I doubted there would be a winner. But as I pulled away from his lips and kissed along his jaw, sinking the fingers of my right hand into his hair and forcing his head to tilt to the side, I realized that if I wanted a power play, I could probably win it.

He whimpered a little, then moaned deeply as I pressed my teeth down on the sensitive skin of his neck, his breathy sounds mixing with mine as his hips thrust forward.

"Fuck." He groaned, one of his hands running down my shirt and unbuckling my jeans to make room to slide underneath. "You've got some size to you..."

I smirked a little, raising an eyebrow. "Would you rather I fucked you?"

"Another time." Quinn chuckled darkly. "For now, I wanna see if I can take it somewhere else."

For a moment, my brain lingered on the phrase, another time. Warning bells tried to go off that maybe this was a bad idea.

What if Quinn really did out me back home?

Those thoughts flew from my head when I felt a wet heat surround my length. Looking down quickly, I saw possibly the most attractive sight I'd ever seen before.

Quinn's mouth was stretched around my cock, very slightly pulled into a smirk as his green eyes watched my reaction. He was clearly well versed in the act as his tongue ran over every sensitive area. My head fell back against the pillow as he pulled moans from my lips over and over. He was too damn good at this.

"Quinn, I didn't bring you here for this," I whined after a short while.

"Feeling impatient?" he asked with a laugh as he pulled back and flashed a smile at me, his eyes filled with such need that I could feel reciprocated through my whole body.

"Yes," I replied instantly.

Quinn laughed. "Well, if you'd tell me where you put your prep stuff, I'd be able to do more than this."

I blinked up at him for a moment before I laughed and shook my head. "The drawer of the left bedside table."

"Gotcha." Once he knew where things were, Quinn took no time in fetching the lube and coating his index and middle finger with it. Pushing my jeans down to my knees, he slid his hand between my legs, and the first finger ran around the edge of my rim before slowly sinking inside.

Taking me apart was something Quinn didn't need much practice with at all. I was soon bare from the waist down, and my shirt unbuttoned so he could bite down on the skin by my ribs, which he had discovered made me shudder and moan.

"You sound good," Quinn whispered into my ear as he pulled his fingers from me. "Roll over."

Normally, I would have argued being told what to do, but I found myself rolling over to my front, my body pliant when Quinn's strong hands pulled at my hips to guide me onto my hands and knees. The sound of the lube bottle and a condom packet ripping made me lick my lips, whimpering in anticipation.

Groaning deeply as Quinn's length pushed inside me, I felt the burn of the stretch and the pulsing heat slowly filling more and more of me. I decided then and there that what they said about big men might have been correct. They weren't just tall...

Pausing once he had pushed in as far as I could take him, Quinn draped himself over my back, kissing, licking, and nibbling at the back of my neck. "You're so fucking hot, Jase." My name on his lips was ambrosia.

As soon as he began to move, all sense was lost. I don't know how many times I moaned his name, I don't know when it was that I ripped the pillowcase with my fingers, and I honestly don't know if we had one round or two before I passed out from exhaustion and pleasure.

CHAPTER EIGHTEEN

Quinn

THE CURTAINS OF the musty old motel room did nothing to keep the sun off of my face the following morning. Normally, I liked basking in the sun, but even with my eyes closed against it, I could feel the light causing my head to pound.

Rolling over with a groan, I stretched out my arm, expecting to find a body, but

I found nothing but empty space and cold sheets.

Bracing myself against the pain, I opened my eyes slowly as the light hit me square in the face like a hot poker. I was alone on the bed, naked except for the top sheet. I glanced around the room. It was completely empty... the only sounds were from outside.

"He left?" I asked no one, letting a sigh leave my lips. As I pushed myself to a seated position, my head swam with a hangover I probably shouldn't have had.

After inspecting the bedside tables, I realized there weren't any of Jase's belongings left. Nor was there a single note to explain why he had gone. I felt disappointed and mildly irritated. I thought we had gotten to a better place the night before, even without the sexual events that followed. The fact he had been willing to get up and leave without a word was slightly hurtful.

With a huff of annoyance, I climbed from the bed to search through my discarded clothes for my phone.

"Fuck!" I groaned in frustration when my gaze landed on the time and the dying battery. I was late for my own checkout, which meant no time to charge my phone either.

"Could have at least woken me as he left, so this didn't cost me extra," I grumbled as I threw on the clothes from the previous night and rushed out the door, and as quickly as I could, made my way back to my hotel.

There was no time to shower. Therefore, I swiftly changed into a casual set of clothes for travel and checked out. I didn't enjoy the concept of sitting in my car for an hour smelling of sex, sweat, and alcohol, but I didn't have much choice.

It still bothered me that Jase had left without a word.

Was he angry?

Was he ashamed?

Did he regret what had happened?

He had definitely invited me back to his room, and he had been the one to ask for more than just a blowjob. I could not remember doing anything that he hadn't asked for... But perhaps it had been adrenaline and alcohol that had fuelled it. I had certainly had nights where I had regretted it, but I at least had the decency to stick around.

Finally, about fifteen minutes from Baton Rouge, I recalled the look of sheer panic that had dawned on his face when he had first seen me at the club.

Perhaps the answer was as simple as Jase had gotten scared when he woke up sober and realized he would actually have to face the man who had fucked him?

It could have been a hard hit from reality that made him freak out and flee before I awoke.

Thinking about it that way, I felt all the irritation in me fade. Now I only wished that he had stayed so I could have ensured he knew this was not something to be afraid of. It was a fun night, but if he never wanted to acknowledge it, then I would respect that. I had no intention of making the closet more difficult for him to be in.

Reaching home was bliss for me. Thinking so much about the situation with a hangover and not much sleep had left me exhausted. I needed food, water, pills, and probably a nap before I would be able to function properly. Jared wasn't in, which meant doing all of that was on the cards, and falling asleep on the couch was acceptable.

After popping two pain pills, followed by scarfing down a few pieces of left over pizza I'd found in the refrigerator, and guzzling a bottle of water, I went straight to the living room, closed the blinds behind me, and flopped onto the sofa face first. The piece of furniture groaned under my weight as I crawled over it, passing out before my head had even reached the other end.

CHAPTER NINETEEN

Quinn

WHEN I WOKE, I could hear the low drone of voices from the television and knew immediately that Jared was home and watching his nature show in silence so he didn't disturb me.

"You had a good night, I take it?" He chuckled once I had stirred enough for him to know I was conscious.

"What?" I asked stupidly, still groggy from sleep.

"You smell of sex, dude." Jared laughed.

I groaned slightly. I had been so tired after having food that I had completely forgotten to shower before falling asleep.

"Sorry," I mumbled as I sat up and blinked drowsily, glancing around the room. It was still light out, but that didn't mean much, as it was summer. It could have been eight in the evening, for all I knew.

"Don't be! I'm glad to know the night was a success."

"Hmm. Not sure about that."

Jared cocked his head to the side as his smile faltered. "What do you mean?"

I hesitated for a moment, unsure how I was going to be able to explain it without outing Jase. Not that Jared knew him or would say anything, but the principle of it was important. I had promised not to tell anyone what I knew, and I intended to keep that promise.

"I bumped into someone I knew," I began slowly. "We had such a laugh, and we ended up sleeping together, but in retrospect, it was probably one of my worst ideas." Even if it wasn't really my idea, sure, I had thought about it, but it was Jase who had acted.

"If you had fun, why was it a bad idea?" Jared ventured.

I sighed heavily before the main thought I had been stuck on for most of the day fell from my lips. "Because I want to do it again."

Jared laughed loudly. "That good?"

"No. Well, yes…" I admitted. "But it's

not just that. I want the laughter, the conversation, and I'd like to actually wake up with him still there so I could make breakfast.

"Careful, sounds like you like the guy." Jared chuckled.

"Yeah, sure." I laughed it off, reminding myself just how long it had been since I had been in a relationship and justifying that that was the reason why I was fantasizing about those things. Usually, the daydreams were fine, but more often than not, I didn't imagine one specific person. Hopefully, the Jase addition to them would fade in time, and work wouldn't become awkward again.

Still, it was near impossible to forget the way Jase had looked spread around my fingers or how delicious his moans were as I drove into him harder than I thought I'd be able to. Once he was relaxed and aroused enough, he had even met my thrusts with each stroke, making the force that I tormented his insides with considerably higher.

It was a miracle I had lasted as long as I had, though I suspected the alcohol had more to do with that than anything.

In the shower ten minutes later, the memories of the night before joined my hand and me in a joyous self-pleasuring session.

CHAPTER TWENTY

Quinn

THE NEXT MORNING, I woke up from a dream of taking Jase against my bedroom door, where he cried out beautifully. By the time I got to work, I wasn't actually sure I would be able to look at him without feeling some kind of arousal.

I was the first to arrive for the shift, which at least meant I could get settled in and help myself to the worst coffee in the world before anyone else arrived. I had to put six sugars in it just to make it tolerable, but I needed something to do while I waited for the previous shift to leave. Otherwise, I was going to drive myself insane.

Carmen greeted me with a nod while Mark and Johnson gave the usual half-assed wave I had become familiar with. It was obvious they had worked with and known Jase for a long time and had his back automatically, even if they didn't know everything. In a way, I respected them for their loyalty, but that didn't mean it didn't piss me off too.

"Morning to you too. Hope you had a nice weekend," I called after them. I realized moments later that I shouldn't have let my irritation out on anyone.

Carmen's raised eyebrow said that much. If I wasn't looking for trouble, I shouldn't go around starting it. I shrugged my shoulders in response and turned back to my locker, which I had decided to deep clean during my wait. My coffee sat on the top of it so I could reach up and have a sip whenever I wanted. Though, every sip made me grimace in disgust.

"I thought I warned you the coffee here was shit?" The laugh that came from behind me was honestly one I didn't think I'd hear again. Turning around, I found myself looking at Jase's amused grin as he pulled a coffee from the carrier tray in his hand and held it out for me to take. "Here."

It wasn't exactly something huge. It wasn't an explanation of his disappearance or any form of acknowledgment that anything had even happened. But it was a very clear sign that Jase didn't hate me for what happened. As he walked away, I felt a tension in my spine release along with confusion.

Had I actually been that worried that Jase was going to hate me?

He had despised me since I stepped foot into this place.

Had one night of laughter really given me that much hope?

Lifting the cup, I took a sip of a sweet, almost buttery-tasting latte. It reminded me of the Buttery Nipples, and I laughed lightly to myself.

Maybe Jase *was* acknowledging what had happened. He just couldn't handle a conversation that was too serious right now. That kind of tone could easily freak anyone out. I understood that.

"Damn, coffees all around. You're in a good mood." Mark laughed.

I couldn't help but look across the locker room and watch what little I could through the open door.

"Bet he got laid while we were off." Johnson nudged Jase in the ribs, careful not to spill his own coffee but laughing loudly when Jase choked slightly on his.

"You're an idiot," Jase grumbled, his cheeks darkening in color.

Damn.

He looked good when he blushed, and honestly, I found I liked that his cheeks grew a deep pink shade at the memory of what we had done together.

"You did! Ha! Was she hot?" Mark demanded.

"Was she good?" Johnson joined in.

"Bet he can't even remember her name...." Carmen's voice sounded from somewhere, sounding half amused and half bored. If the door opening and closing was anything to go by, she had probably just gone out for a smoke to get away from the typical guy talk.

"Oh, ignore her," Mark commented. "Come on, tell us. Was she blonde? You like blondes."

I frowned, a niggling feeling of annoyance in my chest.

"Actually..." Jase sighed. "She had dark hair, nearly black. She was hot as hell. Tall, long legs, muscles, and curves, in the right places. A mouth to die for, if you know what I mean."

The two men whistled and laughed at the comment. I was very glad to be in another room as there was no chance I would be able to hide the triumphant smirk that sat on my face as I continued to clean out my locker. Jase was definitely talking about me. Everything other than the pronouns fit.

They were still asking questions by the time I had finished my work on my locker, and I wandered back through to the main room. Jase quickly turned crimson as I entered, most likely assuming I hadn't heard anything so far.

Anyway," he started. "As it's a damn good day, I figured I would tackle the store room. If you guys need me, I'll be in there."

I almost laughed at the obvious stumble he made trying to turn around and flee the room so fast. It was definitely unfair that someone so hot was also that cute. The thought frustrated me. I was supposed to have gotten this out of my system, not developed some kind of stupid crush.

Shit.

Rolling my eyes at myself, I took a seat away from the others to go over some paperwork Captain Clarke had left for us. The coffee and the wordy rambling papers in front of me were at least able to distract me from the fact I was actually tempted to make Jase blush more.

Unfortunately, the papers and coffee only lasted so long. Quicker than I would have liked, I was walking through the station with the papers in hand to give them back to the Captain. I'd have to give him some feedback as well, but other than a few repeating rambles, the general flow was good.

"So what happened with you and

Quinn?"

I paused as I heard Mark's voice from the male bathroom.

"What do you mean?" Jase replied.

"You brought a coffee for him as well this morning. Since when do you play nice with him?"

Mark had a point. Jase had made it pretty obvious that there was something different between us now. I felt bad eavesdropping, but I couldn't make my feet move. I wanted to know what Jase was going to say. He surely wasn't going to admit what had really occurred.

"I bumped into him at the coffee shop the other day." Jase sounded calm. I wondered if I was about to hear a cover story that he had been rehearsing. "We decided to have a chat and came to an agreement to be civil before we create enough of a war zone that it fucks us over in the field."

"Really?"

"Yeah. I mean, think about it. What happens when we get a serious call out, and we all need to have each other's backs? If he and I are at odds and don't trust each other, it could cost someone their life." Jase sighed. "I still hurt from what happened in school, but it ain't worth destroying my future over."

Having heard enough, I forced myself to walk on through the corridor. If Jase was about to speak more of the personal pain I had caused him, I didn't want to overhear that. I wanted him to talk to me in person so I could try to rectify at least a tiny portion of it.

It was a good cover story, though. Even with trust, this job was dangerous enough.

"You all right, son?" Captain Clarke asked as I climbed to my feet after giving him some feedback about the document.

"Just thinking about New Orleans," I admitted.

His face softened immediately, and he nodded. "It was an absolute tragedy. You know, we have a trained therapist on site to help with stuff like this if you need to speak to him. I can set it up quick and discreet like."

It was touching that he would respond like that. Something in his eyes told me that he had seen the therapist once or twice in his career too.

"I'll think about it. Thanks, Cap."

He didn't press the issue. Instead, he just got up from his chair to give me a clap on my shoulder and tell me that the station had my back before motioning for me to get out of his office.

It was a slow morning, but around midday, we received a call out for a car crash on the highway. I hated callouts like this. Being a firefighter, we were trained to give emergency medical treatment, but that didn't mean it was always successful. We arrived before the ambulance and had to begin cutting a young lady from her car while keeping her neck supported in case there was major damage there. Thankfully, she was the only one injured, so Jase and I were able to focus until the paramedics arrived and got her strapped down with a collar on her so she couldn't move and injure herself further.

"Thank god it wasn't worse," I mumbled as we clambered into the truck.

JASE

"Yeah, I've seen some hellish crashes in my time." Jase sighed. "Makes you think about how short life is."

"It's what prompted me to come out..." I admitted, unsurprised by the raised eyebrow Jase gave me. "I was in a drunken crash when I was at college. My friend was seriously injured, but he pulled through. I had a massive crush on him, and suddenly I didn't want to hide that anymore because what if I missed out on something great?"

"So you told him?"

"Yeah, and he punched me in the face and told me to leave him the hell alone."

Jase's features scrunched up in both horror and disgust. "The fuck?"

I laughed lightly and shrugged. "It wasn't the end of the world. It made me realize I'd rather be rejected for who I actually am than loved for pretending to be something that made me miserable."

"You've got guts," Jase breathed after a moment. "I'm more scared of that punch and rejection than anything else."

"And that's okay," I responded. "Fear can keep us safe."

Jase smiled softly as though he had been worried that he was going to be reprimanded for being in the closet.

"If you ever need someone to talk to though, I can always listen." I flashed him a smile. "We could get it over coffee or something."

Jase arched an eyebrow, his look questioning.

"You know... like we did a couple of days ago?" I prompted.

Jase gaped for a moment before sending a slight glare my way. "You overheard me?"

"I did. Though it may have been practical to let me know the cover story so I didn't blow it for you." I laughed.

"Shut up," he grumbled.

"Hey, I could have asked if the tall, dark-haired beauty was really as good in bed as you were describing earlier." I smirked widely, adding what I knew to be an evil teasing glint in my gaze as Jase turned his attention from the road to look at me in surprise.

"Asshole." Jase laughed as he shook his head and smiled.

He was considerably more relaxed around me. Perhaps it was because I had listened to the story of the girl without batting an eye or correcting him. Perhaps he had a little more faith that I wasn't going to out him.

Finally, I felt like I could actually settle into work and was able to relax and start to fit into the team properly.

Jase was fun to be on the trucks with. We spent a lot of time teasing each other and exchanging banter, much like Jase did with everyone else. But every now and then, I would say something a bit too playful, and a slight blush would creep up Jase's cheeks. Every time it did, I was plagued by the same annoying thoughts that he was just so damn cute for someone so hot.

CHAPTER TWENTY-ONE

Quinn

"ARGH, HE'S DRIVING me insane," I grumbled one evening as I flopped down onto the sofa.

"Who?"

"Jase!"

"Is he still being an asshole?"

"Does being so cute I want to kiss him and so hot I want to fuck him count as being an asshole?" I huffed as my roommate laughed loudly at me.

"Depends. Does he know he's doing it?" Jared asked, sniggering in amusement, and kicking my feet off the edge of the sofa so he could sit down.

"I think he knows he's hot, but I don't think he knows just how crazy he is driving me." I sighed. "I thought sleeping with him as a one-time thing would be fine, get it out of my system type deal, but I really just want to do it again."

Jared paused. "Quinn... was Jase the one you were with when you were in Lafayette?"

My eyes widened as I realized that I'd given myself away and he had figured it out fast. I'd also inadvertently broken my promise and outed Jase, much to my chagrin.

JASE

"So, he's not as straight as you say?"

Rolling my eyes slightly, I finally gave in. "No, he isn't. But he's very much in the closet and determined to stay in it."

"Damn. I'm sorry, man." Jared actually seemed to be sympathetic to my troubles. "Is the fact that you bullied him still a sore point too?"

Letting my head drop forward, I sighed heavily. "God knows, but probably, knowing my luck." I had been trying not to think about it, but there were still many moments when he shrunk back from me as something reminded him of our years in school.

I hated who I used to be. I had been such a stupid, pompous, and arrogant young brat who didn't think about his actions. If they had caused this much pain for Jase, I didn't want to imagine who else was still suffering from the things I had done.

"Okay, we need to get you in a better mindset. Let's go out!" Jared said after a couple of beats.

"I don't want to," I replied with a sigh. For some reason, I couldn't even muster up the energy to dress up and smile.

"Oh, come on. We'll go pig out on some junk food along with some good drinks." Jared nudged at my side in the same way that an annoying child might when they wanted attention. Turning my gaze to him, I made it very clear that I wasn't impressed by the action.

"Can you not?" I deadpanned.

"I know how to annoy you into doing what I want," Jared chuckled. "Sure you want to out-stubborn me?"

For a moment, I debated trying just

that. But I knew that he wasn't about to give in, so I just let out a dramatic sigh and nodded. "Fine, you win. Let me change first."

CHAPTER TWENTY-TWO

Quinn

JARED ALWAYS MANAGED to make having drinks and playing pool a good laugh. He was the life of the party, but he didn't drink much, and his game never dipped. He somehow made friends with other patrons, and I soon found myself laughing easily and drinking my way through more pints than I perhaps should have. After another hour or two, I felt as though I couldn't keep up with Jared's pace any longer and decided to try and get his attention so we could go home.

"Yo, Jar," I slurred as I stumbled over thin air, trying to get through the crowd in the bar. "I think it's time for me to say goodbye."

Jared looked at me and chuckled at the way I swayed on my feet. "Damn, you are drunk," he said as we both laughed.

"Yeah, well, I've had a few too many tonight," I told him as he moved toward the exit so he could open the door for me. "Such a gentleman," I mumbled as we walked out into the night air.

"No need to thank me. You're welcome anytime," Jared replied as he held the door open for me. We walked down the front steps, Jared's arm wrapping around me as I slipped and nearly fell.

"You all right?" he asked me as he steadied me against his side.

"Yes. Thank you." I smiled up at him before I closed my eyes and leaned back against him. "I'm tired."

He pulled me closer to him and then wrapped his arm around my shoulder. "I'm not surprised. Come on, let's get you home."

We were halfway across the street when I heard someone yell out to us from behind. I turned to see who it was but didn't recognize anyone in the crowd. It wasn't until the guy started walking toward us that I realized who he was.

"Quinn, my man!" The guy yelled out as he approached. "How have you been, my friend? Haven't seen you in a while."

Jared looked at me with a questioning

expression. "Who is this guy?"

"This is Harold. Used to go to my dad's church," I said slowly, wondering if I should pull myself away from Jared. I really needed to get home because my head was pounding again, and I just wanted to be alone.

"Oh, wow. Hey, Harold." Jared grinned at him before turning back to me. "I'll walk you home."

"That's some good friendship right there." Harold smiled. "But, I just... eh... wanted to warn you, Quinn. There are some pretty unfavorable rumors going around about you. You may not want to stumble so close to another guy on your way home."

"What?" I frowned at him. "Why? What did I do?"

Harold took a step back and looked me

up and down. "They're saying you sin with men, Quinn. Horrid thing, really. I mean, I was at school with ya. I know you'd never do something that disgusting... but there's a lot of people who are starting to talk."

I felt a prickle of anger in my chest, and even though I couldn't stand straight, I still turned a glare toward Harold. "And what exactly is so disgusting about it?" I snapped at him.

Harold looked shocked for a moment. "It's wrong. It's unnatural."

"Well, no one's asking you to do it..." I grumbled. These were the kinds of things that made people scared to come out. My mind went to my past, where I had said such things to Jase. No wonder he had hated me so. "I *am* gay, Harold. If you've got a problem with it, I'm happy to face you anytime."

Harold's mouth opened and closed like a fish out of water. His whole expression changed, and suddenly he was looking at me like I was the scum on the bottom of his shoe as opposed to an old friend.

"How could you?" he asked, as though he was somehow experiencing a betrayal. "Do you understand how sinful this is?"

The anger inside me flared, and I stepped forward, ready to tell Harold just what I thought of him. But Jared's hand on my arm stopped me, and I saw the look in his eye. It was one of warning. Not to fight with Harold but to put up a fight in another way. There was a gleaming look of mischief in his eyes that gave me an idea of exactly what other way the man was thinking.

Well, he was the one with a partner to

explain it to later.

"Well, if it's that sinful, maybe you'll be corrupted if you stay and watch," Reaching out a hand, I sealed my fingers around Jared's shirt and pulled him to me, catching his lips with my own and kissing him hard.

Harold's eyes bulged out of his skull as I kissed Jared so hard he couldn't even speak or react much. I don't know why I did it. Maybe I was angry at the world, maybe I was drunk, or maybe I just wanted to show Harold that I just didn't care what he and the church thought of me anymore.

Once I had heard Harold storm off, I released Jared from my grip and smiled awkwardly at him. "I hope that's what that mischievous look was suggesting."

"Actually, I was going to suggest you

kissed him, but that worked too." Jared laughed loudly, clapping me on the back and then catching me as I stumbled from the force of it.

"Okay, Drinkerella. Home to bed." Jared chuckled. "You need your rest."

I nodded, turning to head home. "Yeah, I think I better do that. Thanks for helping me."

"My pleasure," Jared replied as we finally made it through the front door.

I stumbled into my room and fell face first across my bed without even taking my shoes off. My last thought before I passed out was how I was going to regret drinking so much in the morning.

CHAPTER TWENTY-THREE

Jase

I HAD NOT expected to see Quinn out in town that warm summer night. It was after a long day shift, and from previous conversations, I knew he preferred to stay home. But there he was, standing by the bar with his back turned to me in conversation with his friend, who was laughing at something he'd said. My suspicions were confirmed when Quinn turned around, smiling so easily at the man he was with.

Was he on a date?

The very idea of it had an ill sense of jealousy bubbling up within me. While I didn't have anything against the two of them being together or even having a relationship, as long as they made sure not to involve me, it just seemed wrong for him to be with someone else, knowing how much I cared about him.

Wait.

He didn't know.

I had specifically made sure I kept any and all thoughts and feelings under control since our night together. I needed to keep my distance if I wanted things to remain platonic between us.

But now that he was getting close to

another man, could I really let this go without saying something?

What would happen if I did?

No.

He was a bully and an asshole. I didn't want to be with him anyway.

Deciding to get out of the bar and head to another for the night to get away from the annoying circle of thoughts in my head, I soon bumped into an old friend from school. "Hey there, Callie," I greeted her happily, trying to push any thoughts of Quinn out of my mind.

"Oh my god, Jase! Hi!" She was a perky woman with a short pixie cut and a smile that had always been cute but a little lopsided. Her crooked teeth gave her face character, making her seem more approachable than most. "How are you? You look happy."

"Yeah. Things are good," I lied.

"You're a firefighter these days, aren't you?" Callie asked.

I nodded. "That's right. Been there almost ten years now."

Callie looked impressed. "Wow, so you pretty much went in straight after high school?"

"Well, I had a few years of changing jobs to see what I liked, but yeah," I admitted.

"I'm glad you found your calling. This is such a cool job. I ended up teaching." She laughed. "And now I drink more than I should admit."

We chatted for a while before she left me to go to her next destination. As I walked down the street alone, I couldn't help but think of Quinn again. The thought of him with another man made me feel jealous, angry, and strangely... excited. Though I knew I shouldn't be thinking about him like that, especially given how I felt about him, I just couldn't stop myself.

What am I doing?

Why am I jealous?

I shook the thoughts from my head. I should just go home.

As I rounded a corner, lost in my own thoughts, I spotted Quinn and his friend again. They were walking close, the man's arm around Quinn to keep him close.

Did they just leave the same place?

How long had they known each other?

Why was he paying attention to him instead of me?

I paused, knowing if I walked at my pace, I would end up having to acknowledge them. For a moment, I debated walking the long way home when I saw Quinn being approached by a man I had never liked.

Harold Wright.

He had been one of Quinn's friends in school, and he had been even worse of a bully. If anyone had ever crossed him, he would make their life a living hell.

He was tall, broad-shouldered, and had the kind of greasy hair that only comes from regular use of styling products. His eyes were brown, though the yellow hue of the streetlights made them look otherworldly and evil. He wore a Fred Perry polo shirt and lacrosse jeans with Timberlakes adorning his feet. He was a man of money and it was obvious he took good care of himself, having muscles that bulge through his shirt that I could see from across the street.

JASE

Whatever he was talking to Quinn about obviously wasn't pleasant. I could see the discomfort and anger in my coworker. Quinn's whole body was tense and even though I couldn't see his face, I knew his expression was probably tight while he tried to keep himself calm. A large part of me yearned to go over and comfort him.

But I didn't.

Instead, I watched.

Quinn gave a terse response, which I could hear even though I couldn't see his face. Then, he turned, and my heart sank. His lips slamming against the man he had been laughing with earlier sent lightning pain racing through my chest. My mouth dropped open, and I felt the sharp twinge of jealousy and hurt.

Why was he kissing another guy like

that?

I quickly moved away, heading back the way I came. Not wanting to watch anymore, I tried to shake off my emotions.

Who cares if he kissed that asshole? It wasn't my business.

Right?

CHAPTER TWENTY-FOUR

Jase

THE REST OF the weekend passed in a blur. I did my best to pretend I hadn't seen Quinn in public with another man. I knew it was wrong, but I couldn't help but feel a little wounded. I knew there was nothing actually between Quinn and me, and yet, I still felt rejected.

I spent Sunday in bed, alone, watching

TV. Monday morning, I got up early, showered, and drove to work. I walked in, relieved to find the locker room empty. I didn't have the energy to deal with anyone right now.

I caught sight of myself in a mirror set next to the shower stall. My hair was still wet from my shower at home, so it looked even more like I'd been dragged through a jungle by wild dogs. My eyes were rimmed with dark circles and my skin was pasty white and covered in dry patches. I couldn't believe how bad I felt... especially after sleeping all last night. It must have been a really shitty night. I was glad I couldn't remember if I had any dreams on top of the frustrating thoughts of Quinn with another man. I pulled on my uniform and grabbed a cup of coffee before heading out into the hall.

JASE

"Jase! Hey, didn't wake up early enough to stop in for the good stuff?" Johnson asked, motioning to the coffee that everyone knew I hated.

I shrugged. "I had a rough night," I lied.

"Ah, yeah. I hear ya." He nodded. "Hopefully, the day makes it better."

I had to work with Quinn, so I doubted that there would be any kind of plus to the day. Especially if he decided to tell me about his boyfriend. The idea of hearing about someone else kissing him made me want to scream, even though I knew it shouldn't. It did.

"Morning, Jase. Good morning, Johnson," Quinn greeted us as we walked down the hall.

"Good morning, Quinn," I returned, trying to ignore the twinge of guilt I felt every time I thought about what I'd seen and how I was reacting internally.

Just because he has a boyfriend doesn't mean I can't be happy for him.

Or does it?

It was almost lunchtime when Quinn walked past me toward the break room. He stopped and gave me a quick smile. "Hey, Jase."

I smiled back. "You have a good weekend?"

"Yeah, thanks. You?" he asked, turning to look at me. There was an awkward pause where neither of us said anything.

"Um…" I stammered, unable to come up with something to say. "Yeah, good."

"Okay then. See you later, all right?" He turned to walk away.

I looked after him, feeling a bit

disappointed that our conversation was over so quickly. He seemed distracted, and I wondered if his mind was preoccupied. I let myself think that maybe he wasn't thinking about his boyfriend at all but rather me. That he was interested in me too.

I knew it was wishful thinking, but I hoped anyway.

This was getting ridiculous. But more than that, I found myself jealous of how both Quinn and the other man had been able to just show their desire in public. Doing that was everything I wanted but everything I feared. I'd never acted on my desires before because I didn't want anyone to know about them.

And even if they did know, what would they think?

Would they tell others?

Would people laugh at me for thinking such things?

Would they judge me as a pervert or worse?

It wasn't worth the risk. Besides, it wasn't like I hadn't made out with girls before... But it had just felt so wrong.

Anything with girls always felt wrong. Even when my mother spoke about a young lady she had met at her yoga class.

"I think you'd really like her," my mother said to me over dinner one night. "She's very sweet but has a wicked sense of humor."

My mother always seemed to have these mysterious friends who were 'very sweet' and who she told me about every time we talked on the phone. It was rare for her to bring them up over dinner in person, though. Most of the time, I ended up feeling like I should duck and cover to avoid any further talk.

I thought about meeting the girl just to satisfy my mother. But the image of Quinn kissing that other man flashed into my mind, followed by the memory of how he had kissed me at the club and the way his muscles seemed to shine with a small layer of sweat when we had slept together. The fact that he did not make me feel dirty only made my thoughts about him all the more confusing. I knew nothing could ever come from it... but my mouth opened before I could think anything through.

"Mom, I can't keep meeting up with girls. I'm gay. It'll never work out," I said, a sad and defeated tone overlapping the words.

Time seemed to freeze. My mother

stared at me for a few seconds while I waited for a retort, some form of denial or anger that would indicate my honesty had been wrong. She was silent. Then she stood up and took my hand in hers.

"I don't care if you're gay..." she said simply.

I looked up in surprise, searching her face, which went from calm to mildly annoyed.

"Did you really think I would care? Boy, how little do you think of me?" she asked sternly, looking down at me.

"No, Mom! Of course, you wouldn't care," I replied, suddenly wondering where I had even got myself concerned that she would. She had always been a supportive and caring woman.

She paused again, trying to find the right words, then smiled.

"You're right. You should have said something sooner. I feel bad having tried to set you up with so many women." She reached over and patted my cheek. "I'll just have to find a nice man for you instead."

I laughed at the idea of my mother trying to set me up with a man. But I couldn't help but smile back at her. I loved the woman, despite her oddities.

"Maybe there's someone at work?" she suggested with a raised eyebrow. "Firefighters are usually cute."

I blushed a little, ducking my head and taking a large mouthful of the apple pie she had brought out.

"Oh, there is... What's he like?"

"Taken," I grumbled, watching her face fall into something akin to sympathy.

"Oh, love. I'm sorry," she said,

reaching over and placing a hand on mine. "It's hard to meet men without being obvious about your interests."

I sighed a little, feeling a bit embarrassed now that I had admitted to her that I was gay. "He knows I'm gay. He is too. But I've seen him with another guy, so I guess I'm a bit late to the scene."

"Well, if he didn't wait for you, then he isn't the one," Mom said.

I chuckled at her idealism.

"So, you are telling me Dad was *The One* for you?" I chuckled, glancing at the back door. As usual, Dad had vacated the table as soon as he had finished his meal and taken his dessert and a beer into his workshop.

"He has his moments where I wonder," Mom laughed. "But I do love him with everything I am."

My smile faltered slightly. "How do you think he'll take the news?"

"Oh, you leave the old grump to me. He'll be fine." She flashed me a reassuring smile before finishing off her pie.

I rolled my eyes, amused at the way she tried to pretend everything was normal.

CHAPTER TWENTY-FIVE

Jase

I SPENT MOST of the rest of the week working. It was harder than expected to stay away from Quinn and the memories we made together. I kept thinking of the things he'd whispered to me, the way he smelled, the way his skin felt against mine. We had such a good time together. And yet I was still conflicted about what he meant to me.

Was it lust?

Or something else entirely?

On Friday night, I practically crawled into my house after a long shift at the fire station. I was exhausted, but I couldn't stop thinking about Quinn. I wanted to see him again outside of work.

But what would happen if I did see him?

Would he reject me?

Stumbling into the bathroom, I turned on the water, allowing it to heat while I stripped down, tossing the dirty clothes into the hamper.

Stepping under the hot spray, I sighed as the water beat down on my sore muscles, my mind wandering back to the night with Quinn and my dick hardening instantly.

JASE

I grabbed some body wash, running my hand over my pecs and down my abdomen until I fisted my already hard cock, a moan slipping from my lips as memories flitted through my brain.

My body going pliant when Quinn's strong hands pulled at my hips to guide me onto my hands and knees. The sound of the lube bottle and a condom packet being ripped open and making me whimper in anticipation.

Groaning deeply as Quinn's hard length pushed inside me and I felt the burn of the stretch and the pulsing heat slowly filling more and more of me.

Quinn pausing once he had pushed in as far as I could take him, draping himself over my back, kissing, licking, and nibbling at the back of my neck. Pressing his lightly furred chest flush against my back as he whispered my name in my ear, making me cum again and again.

I moaned his name, my breath catching in my chest as I felt my release build up within me, pulling my balls up tight, heat rushing through my belly before long, thick ropes of cum painted the shower walls, mixing with the water and swirling down the drain.

Just as I stepped from the shower, tying a fresh towel around my hips, my phone dinged from across the room, and I quickly jogged over and snatched it up. My heart fluttered as I saw that it was a text from Quinn, with an invitation to come hang out at his place.

What were the odds?

CHAPTER TWENTY-SIX

Quinn

WELL, I'D DONE it. Inviting Jase to my place had been a challenging thing to do. I was very nervous about being behind closed doors with him, without anyone else around.

Jared had agreed to go to a friend's for the evening so I could have some space. We'd stayed up talking until well after midnight most nights since our night out and the backlash I had received from the church and my parents. Eventually, Jared convinced me to try to see if anything could develop with Jase. He said he wanted me to be happy and that he would support whatever decision I made. So, I texted Jase the next day and invited him over. I was honestly surprised he agreed.

I decided on an old-fashioned spaghetti bolognese. It's one of my favorite meals and a true comfort food from my past. I'd also baked some bread earlier in the week as part of my new healthy eating kick, so I rustled that up into a loaf of garlic bread to go with the meal.

Shortly before Jase was due to arrive, I began second-guessing myself. I had put on one of my nicer shirts and a pair of tight black jeans that left little to the imagination... but I hadn't said anything about a date in the text.

What if Jase thought we were just going to hang out as friends?

Would he think I was being too forward or pushy?

Ugh, what if he didn't come?

I tried my best not to freak out, but it did make me feel a bit nauseous while I quickly changed into pants that didn't scream, 'Yes, I have size down here, and I want you to know it'.

CHAPTER TWENTY-SEVEN

Quinn

JASE ARRIVED RIGHT on time. I opened the door and let him in. His eyes lit up when he saw all the food I had prepared for us. "Wow, this is amazing," he exclaimed. "I was expecting takeout. I didn't know you cooked."

"It's not my greatest talent, but I can make a few dishes really well." I rubbed the back of my neck shyly, unsure why I was so nervous tonight.

Actually, that was a lie. I knew exactly why I was nervous. This was the first time since New Orleans I had actually wanted to try and have something date-like with someone.

"I've never been much of a cook myself," he admitted. "My family are very good cooks though, my Mom especially. She taught me to make a lot of their recipes, but I've only really succeeded with her apple pie" He smiled fondly.

We sat down at the table and started chatting away. After a couple of minutes, I noticed he was watching me out of the corner of his eye. "What?" I asked suddenly.

He gave me a sheepish smile, looking down at the table. "Nothing..." he mumbled.

I frowned and cocked my head to the side.

"I guess I just expected something different?" He shrugged.

"What, like take out, beer, weights, and some porn videos on the shelves?" I laughed loudly as a look of guilt flashed across Jase's eyes. "Oh wow. Do I come across as that much of a stereotype?"

Jase grimaced. "Kinda? You come across as everything I pretend to be. All manly and nothing much to second guess."

"You don't have to act tough for me," I told him softly.

He looked up and met my gaze. "No, I do."

"Why?" I arched an eyebrow as I watched difficult emotions shine from him.

"Because if I'm not tough with everyone, then I'll let slip where I'm not supposed to."

Ah.

Yes, I knew that fear well.

Setting my fork down for a moment, I reached over the table to tap his forehead so those gorgeous eyes met mine. "You can be tough and gay. My ex taught me that."

"You've been in a normal relationship?" he asked, clearly intrigued.

"Yeah. It was awesome. Didn't last, though, but we are still really good friends."

"In New Orleans?"

I nodded as Jase asked his question.

"Do you see them much now?" Something about his voice was tight, as though he was holding something back.

"No." I sighed. "I can't."

"Why?" He looked at me carefully.

"Do you know what happened at my last station, Jase?" I asked, though I knew full well that none of my new team knew about it. I figured they would have treated me very differently if they did.

Jase's eyebrows furrowed in confusion, obviously thinking this was a strange change of topic. But, still, he shook his head. "I don't, no."

"Someone committed arson on a warehouse, and the only reason I survived was because my ex was there to help me. We worked together. He was my partner."

Jase's eyes went wide. "Holy shit. Did he..."

"He died in that fire, along with every single one of my other teammates. I was the only one who made it out." I felt the grief I kept so tightly under wraps well up in my chest, making it hard to breathe. Tears threatened from behind my eyes.

Jase was looking at me with heartache and terror in his eyes. I hated it when people heard the story because there was always so much pity and so many apologies for my loss.

"Did they catch who did it?" Jase asked. Not a question I usually got straight away. Usually, it took a while for the details to filter through.

"They found out who set the fire," I answered. "But they never tracked him down."

"Fucker," Jase growled, causing me to chuckle.

"My thoughts exactly."

"It sounds like you were very close with

him."

"Very," I agreed. "We weren't just partners. We were best friends. The only real thing that ever made me feel safe or happy was him. He's the main reason I came out to the family because I hoped they'd meet him one day."

Jase's eyes were sad as he watched me speak.

Was he just feeling sorry for me?

Or could I be selfish enough to think that maybe he would like to be more important than that to me one day?

"Why did you break up?" Jase asked tentatively.

"We both quickly realized we were forcing a romantic love onto what was actually a deep solid friendship." I smiled. "We didn't understand just how many kinds of love there were... but I realized I wanted the whole shebang. Romance, sexual intimacy, laughter, closeness, trust. The whole thing."

"And you didn't think he felt the same?"

"No," I sighed. "He wasn't someone who was into romance and didn't ever think he would be."

"I can't understand that," Jase commented. "I'm scared of it, but I would love to hold hands in public and give someone flowers."

I laughed. Yeah, I could see why I was so drawn to this man. "Oh yeah? What kind of flowers would you want?"

"Promise not to laugh?" Jase pointed the finger at me as he cleared his plate. "Peonies. They are considered a sign of good luck and a happy marriage."

I snorted. "You're such a dork."

JASE

"Oh, shut up. I bet your flower choice wouldn't be any better," Jase grumbled.

"Hmm. Not, probably not. I actually like snapdragons." I shrugged and chuckled as Jase raised an eyebrow my way. "I know, strange choice, right."

"Not exactly cliché." Jase smirked and then leaned back in his chair, crossing his arms over his chest as he watched me.

"Well, I'm not exactly normal." I flashed him a grin.

CHAPTER TWENTY-EIGHT

Quinn

"WANT A DRINK?" I asked, picking up his empty plate and stacking it onto mine so I could clear the table.

"Sure, what do you have?" Jase asked.

"Well, beer." I chuckled at the earlier expectations Jase had voiced. "But we've also got some raspberry vodka which is very good with lemonade, whiskey, honey mead, and some peppermint schnapps somewhere." I opened a cabinet to show him the various alcohol bottles within.

Jase's eyes went wide in response to that list. "Holy shit!" He looked around again as if he expected someone to suddenly appear with a tray of drinks and snacks. "Where did you get all this?"

"My roommate tends to get given booze as presents from everyone but doesn't actually drink much," I explained, picking out the raspberry vodka for myself. "So we keep it here so we can have it when people come over."

He nodded understandingly. "I see." Then his eyes narrowed slightly as they focused on something behind me. "Is that a unicorn gin?"

I turned around to look where he was looking and found him pointing at a bottle labeled 'Unicorn Gin' sitting among the other bottles. "Yes..." I said slowly, thinking about how to explain what it really was. "We have yet to touch it."

"We should try it." He laughed, flashing me a cocky grin. "It sounds sickly."

"That's because it's not meant to be consumed neat." I flashed him a smile. "You need ice with it or something to make it taste better."

"Maybe." He shrugged and then pointed to another shelf. "Tell you what, I'll have an Elvis juice ale, please." He motioned to the cans at the back of the cupboard.

"Coming right up." I smiled, grabbing a couple of the cans and leading Jase through to the living room. He sat down on one of the couches and looked around curiously while I set the drinks down on the coffee table in front of him.

He snapped open the lid on the first drink, his eyes narrowing slightly as he sniffed it before taking a sip. "This tastes weird…" He frowned after swallowing the first mouthful. "But interesting."

I snorted, smiling at him. "Good?"

His eyes widened a little at my tone. "Yeah." He reached for his second drink. "The thing is…it doesn't taste like I thought it would." His eyes were bright and clear as he stared at me. "Elvis juice sounds like it should be… I don't know… salty?"

I laughed loudly at the obvious innuendo. "No, no saltiness." I shook my head, grinning at him. "It's just a fruity-tasting lager, you silly man."

Jase laughed a little and settled back

on the sofa. "Let's call it an American IPA beer and leave it at that." He grinned at me. "So, um, what do we do now?"

I raised an eyebrow at the sudden change in topic. "What did you think we'd do?"

He shrugged. "Whatever you wanted to do?"

I rolled my eyes and leaned forward to rest my elbows on my knees. "Well, if you want to watch TV, there are a few things on at the moment. We could also play video games."

"Video games?" Jase repeated, shaking his head. "I didn't think you'd be into those."

"I'm not." I sighed theatrically. "But, sometimes, when my roommate goes out, I feel like I have to entertain myself somehow."

"Oh." He seemed to consider this. "I guess that makes sense, then. Though I think a movie is probably a good call. Have you got any good sci-fi films?"

"Sure." I nodded. "We've got a lot of them." I gestured toward the cupboards fulled with Dvds around me. "You can take your pick."

Jase picked one out, and handed it to me with a grin. It was a movie I hadn't seen before, so I wasn't sure how I felt about it. But I knew Jase would enjoy it, so I couldn't complain.

As the film started, I noticed a small smile playing across Jase's lips. He looked relaxed and happy as he drank his beer and munched on the snacks I'd brought out. I liked seeing him like this.

CHAPTER TWENTY-NINE

Quinn

"WOW, THAT WAS intense," Jase murmured. "Who directed it? That guy's good."

I shook my head in amusement. "It was only his third feature film." I pointed out. "I'm surprised you haven't heard of him, it's been getting rave reviews everywhere lately."

"Huh. I must live under a rock." Jase chuckled. "I'll have to check him out online later."

I smiled lightly as he jotted the name down on his phone. I noticed that we had moved closer together during the movie. I thought about asking him if he minded if I put my arm around his shoulder, but I hesitated. I wasn't sure whether he might find it too intimate, even though I wouldn't mind doing it.

In the end, I decided against it. Instead, Jase said something I had not expected. "I came out to my Mom."

I turned to him with wide eyes. "Really? Did it go okay?"

"She told me she loved me regardless of who I am," he explained. "And then she hugged me tight." He smiled warmly. "We decided to not tell my father yet, though.

He's an old traditional Texan, so Mom is going to work on him for me."

"That's amazing!" I exclaimed. "Congratulations! Your mom seems really cool. I'm somewhat jealous. I wish my mother had taken such a viewpoint." I sighed. "Mine hasn't talked to me for a few weeks now."

"Why don't you talk to her?" Jase asked, concern darkening his expression.

"I've tried," I replied, my voice soft and sad. "She's blocked my number since it became public knowledge that I'm gay. Seems now that everyone at the church knows about it, I've been pushed out."

I was surprised when Jase leaned forward and wrapped his arms around my shoulders, and pulled me into a hug. I leaned my cheek against his chest and inhaled deeply, feeling his warmth. "I'm so sorry, Quinn," he whispered softly. "Is there anything I can do?"

I shook my head. "No, I don't suppose there is." I rested my head back against his shoulder. "I just need to get over it."

Jase stroked my hair gently. "I know it's hard, but you're a strong guy. You'll make it through this."

I nodded slowly. "Thanks, Jase."

He gave me a little squeeze. "If you ever want to talk, I'm here."

I smiled wryly. "I know. I'll definitely take you up on that."

As I pulled back, I realized just how close his face was to mine. His lips were inches away from mine, and I could smell the scent of beer on his breath. I felt a sudden heat begin to burn inside me, and my heart beat faster.

My hand was still on his shoulder,

holding him in place as he held me. Slowly, I moved my gaze up to meet his eyes. They were full of warmth and desire, and his lips parted slightly on their own accord. I saw the intensity of his feelings mirrored in my own, and I was suddenly filled with the urge to kiss him.

I found myself leaning forward, bringing our lips together tenderly. At first, he resisted, but after a moment, he followed suit and closed his mouth over mine. We kissed tentatively at first, but the longer we did it, the more passionate it became.

Our tongues danced gently against each other, tasting each other's flavor. I felt a surge of excitement run through me as my hands explored his body. My fingers traced the muscles of his shoulders, feeling them tighten under my touch. Then I slid my hands down his chest, feeling his warm skin beneath my fingertips. As my hands reached his waistband, he lifted one arm to wrap around my shoulder. The contact sent electricity zinging through me, shivers racing down my spine.

His tongue finally entered my mouth, making me moan softly. It wasn't long before I felt him move his other arm so that they both wrapped around my shoulders. The more passion we expressed, the more I wanted him to do it again. After kissing for several minutes, I pulled back with a smile on my lips and looked into his eyes. "Want to go to the bed?" I asked him.

Jase nodded and let me lead him by the hand, pulling him up the stairs behind me. Once there, I turned to face him. He was looking at me with a serious expression and I worried he was having second thoughts.

"You okay? You have any questions or concerns about this?"

"No, never," Jase said quickly.

I smiled at him and slowly began unbuttoning my shirt. For some reason, I didn't want to look away from his eyes. His gaze seemed to be focusing intently on my chest, which only made me feel even better. When he finally tore his eyes away from my chest, he gazed into my eyes once more, this time with an almost pleading look.

I gave him a gentle smile and then slid my hand under his shirt to feel the smooth skin of his abdomen. He gasped when I touched him, and I could see his erection growing in his pants. This wasn't what I had planned. I hadn't actually *planned* anything, in fact. But something about Jase just set me on fire and I couldn't control the desire and heat that I felt as soon as his lips touched mine.

Slowly, I removed my hand from his stomach and moved down his body. I could feel his breathing getting heavier as I went further down. By the time I reached his belt, he was practically gasping for air. I unhooked his belt and undid his button. I heard him gasp as I took his zipper down.

A smirk pulled on my lips as I slid my fingers beneath the waistband of his boxers and cradled his dick. He was already half-hard, and I knew that it would grow even more if I continued to touch him. I slid my hand back up and then ran it along the length of his shaft, causing him to groan and shudder.

Grasping the waistband again, I slipped his boxers off of his hips. His cock sprang free, springing toward me like a hungry predator. I stared at it for a moment, mesmerized by the sight. It was thick and long, standing out from his body. The head was dark red, and I could see the veins running through it. I dipped my head to take the tip between my lips.

Jase moaned and leaned his head against the wall behind him. I could feel his hands grip the back of my neck tightly as I sucked on him. I began bobbing my head, sucking him deeper and deeper.

"Oh, fuck!" His voice was muffled when he spoke.

I smiled around his dick and then took more of him into my mouth. He was still wearing his clothes, and I had to remove his belt properly before I could pull his jeans down further to give me full access to him. Once I got them off of his feet, I kicked them aside and resumed giving him pleasure.

His legs trembled, and he had difficulty holding himself up. I felt his fingers tighten in my hair, holding my head closer while he chased the pleasure I gave him. I began moving my mouth faster, taking him deeper each time I sank down onto him. I felt him throb in my mouth, and I could hear him moaning as I worked.

When I felt him tense, I pulled him out and licked the tip. He sighed and pushed my head back down. With a sudden burst, he came all over my cheeks and chin, covering me with his hot seed. I swallowed eagerly, licking him clean. I loved the taste of his cum.

"Don't stop," he gasped, and I smiled.

I rose up and kissed him again, tasting the salty residue left from his orgasm. His cock was still hard as steel, and I could tell that he was ready for more. I didn't hesitate to kiss him again. I grabbed his hand and led him further into the bedroom, pushing him onto the bed. Then I climbed on top of him and straddled his lap.

"You're going to make me come again," he said, smiling at me.

I laughed and brushed the hair from his eyes. "That's the idea." I chuckled wickedly.

CHAPTER THIRTY

Jase

I SUCKED IN a breath of anticipation at the wicked chuckle. His eyes promised a pleasure I could only dream of.

"I'm going to fuck you, Jase." He sat up and grabbed my thighs. Leaning forward, he kissed me with an intensity that stole my breath. "This time, I want to see your face when you come for me."

There was something in the back of my mind saying that I shouldn't be doing this with Quinn again. But whatever it was, it was lost in the haze of want and pleasure that I felt as he began to unbuckle his belt. Pulling down his jeans, he kicked them off before sitting back down between my legs again. A rush of cold air filled the space left by his movement, and I shivered from the sensation. The bulge in his boxers was obvious, a small damp patch showing just how turned on he had become from sucking me off.

Fuck.

A man who enjoyed giving just as much as he enjoyed getting himself off. It would take a lot of self-control not to reach over and tug him out into the open.

Quinn's fingers were slick and warm against the skin of my inner thigh as they massaged my skin before his lips trailed after them. Biting and nipping at the sensitive skin, I could feel his stubble brushing against my length, stimulating and tormenting me to a half-hard state.

"Quinn…" I whimpered. I hadn't noticed the way he had reached to his bedside for lube, and so it surprised me when his fingers began tormenting my hole. But there was something about the warmth and wetness that made me relax as he pushed two fingers inside. My whole body clenched tight around him as I tried to stifle the cries that tore through me.

"Shhh," he hushed against my mouth and then slid his other hand over my rigid cock. "I want you to get ready for what's coming."

Fuck.

I didn't know if it was the pain or the

pleasure that was making my head spin.

Quinn's fingers moved faster and deeper inside me. He added a third finger before using his other hand to start stroking my shaft. I knew he was only trying to prepare my ass for what was to come. But that didn't stop me from coming undone. Waves of pleasure crashed over my body, and I let out a guttural moan as Quinn found the sensitive bundle of nerves within me.

"You're so fucking beautiful," he growled against my throat.

His words sent a shudder through my body. "Please... please, don't tease me like this..."

He chuckled against my neck before moving up and kissing my lips. "I won't tease you unless you ask me to."

And all I wanted was *more*. That was

the problem. So many times, I'd been close to begging him to fuck me. But every time I thought about asking, I knew I couldn't do it. I wasn't sure how I could be intimate with him without feeling guilty.

Why was I feeling guilty?

My mind flickered with the image of the man I had seen Quinn kissing in the street.

Oh.

Shit.

Yeah. This would be cheating.

Or maybe they weren't together properly yet, and I still had a chance to win him over?

The thought should have made me laugh. Instead, my heart sank. There was no way I could compete with someone else. Not only was I a pathetic middle-aged man stuck in the closet, but the guy I had seen in the club was gorgeous.

"I want you so badly," Quinn whispered into my ear, his breath sending shivers down my spine. He sounded genuine, and his eyes were filled with awe as though I was the most beautiful thing he had ever witnessed.

Lifting my hips, I guided him toward my entrance. I wanted to give him everything. Every part of me, my mind, and my soul. I couldn't say no to a face like that. If there was still a chance I could have him, then I should take it.

It took a moment of pressure before I felt him pushing inside. I moaned as he stretched me wide open. "Yes... Oh fuck... Ungh"

I gasped as he settled inside me. His whole length was buried deep inside me, and I felt myself stretch to accommodate him. It hurt, and it felt amazing. We both groaned as he began to move, slowly at first, before building speed and force. Every thrust was met by a gasp or a moan from me. The constant rocking motion was enough to send waves of pleasure rippling through my body. I gripped onto his arms, digging my nails into his flesh.

"Jase... Don't hold back," he begged as I tightened my grip around his muscular shoulders.

I shook my head. "I can't. I want to feel this... so bad."

As soon as I said the words, he began to move harder and faster. I heard myself screaming his name as we came together, our bodies pressed tightly against each other. Quinn kept on moving until he finally came to rest against my chest.

I buried my face into the crook of his neck and breathed him in. He smelled divine, of sweat and spice. I kissed the top of his head and whispered, "That was amazing."

He pulled away and looked down at me. "Thank you."

I smiled up at him. "For what?"

"Everything."

I laughed. "Vague, much."

He grinned. "Sorry. But honestly, thank you. You've given me more pleasure than I've ever experienced in my life."

I blushed at the statement, my heart lightening at the idea. If I had really been able to give him something so good, maybe I could actually have this. Maybe we could have a relationship.

Kissing the tip of his nose, I asked, "I feel like we should have coffee and then go for another round?"

His eyes twinkled with mischief as he slid his length from me. "We can do that... Black with two sugars, right?"

I nodded, unable to help the grin spreading across my face. "Sounds perfect." Pulling my boxers back on and adjusting the shirt he hadn't gotten around to removing from my shoulders, I followed him through the apartment.

As he switched the coffee maker on, he pulled me close to him to steal kisses while we waited. When he finally turned around and handed me a mug, I tried not to stare at his near-naked body. A quick glance confirmed that he was completely hard again under his boxers.

"Wow..." I whispered.

He shrugged. "You're too tasty for your own good."

A blush crept into my cheeks at the compliment. I sipped my coffee before I heard the front door open.

"Oh God," I groaned as I covered my mouth with my hand. It was the guy who Quinn had been kissing in the street. He had a set of keys in his hands, and he obviously lived here too. His dark hair fell over one eye, and he wore a white shirt with some kind of blue tie underneath.

"Shit."

I glanced at Quinn's obvious state, walking around in just his boxers, and then down at myself in an open shirt and boxers with hair that clearly looked as though I had been fucked thoroughly.

By Quinn.

In the apartment that these two shared.

Quinn wasn't just taken...

JASE

He was living with the guy.

Mortification and anger flooded through me. I wanted to run, but my feet were rooted to the ground. All I could do was watch as the man walked further inside and closed the door behind him. I watched as he flipped the lock on the door, and then he headed for the bathroom as though we weren't even there.

Fuck this.

I turned a glare at Quinn. "What the fuck is wrong with you?"

Confusion marred his expression, but I didn't stop to talk about it further. Tossing my half-filled coffee mug at him, I stormed through the apartment to grab my trousers and pull them on before picking up my phone and turning for the front door.

"Jase? What's wrong?" Quinn asked, trying to reach out to take my arm as I walked past him.

I snatched his wrist from the air, my fist locked around his wrist so that he couldn't touch me. He pulled back and stepped away quickly. "Don't ever fucking call me again." I pushed the door open and practically ran down the stairs.

"Wait!" Quinn called after me.

I ignored him.

The guy who had come home hadn't blocked my car with his, thankfully. I got in and slammed the door shut before I started the engine. I just needed to get away.

Away from him.

Away from everything.

I needed to be alone.

I needed to think.

CHAPTER THIRTY-ONE

Jase

I DROVE STRAIGHT to my apartment, trying not to stomp loudly as I rushed up the stairs, though I did slam my door behind me a little too heavily for the time of night.

Kicking my shoes angrily from my feet into the entrance hall wall, I grabbed my head in my hands and let out a long, muffled cry of anger. Needing to scrub off his heavenly scent, I rushed through to the bathroom.

I stripped naked and hopped in the shower, letting the hot water wash over me. I didn't cry or scream. I just stood there, hoping to just melt away into the tiles.

How could I have been so stupid?

Why didn't I even ask about the other man?

Had I truly been that desperate to feel Quinn again?

Was all this just a massive mistake?

When the hot water eventually ran out, I stepped out of the shower and dried myself with rough towels. Even though it was late, I knew sleeping tonight wasn't going to happen. I couldn't sleep knowing Quinn was at home, possibly getting ready for bed as I sat here stewing in the aftermath of my own stupidity.

I padded quietly through my bedroom and grabbed my phone. I wasn't going to text him.

Not now.

Maybe not ever.

My anger overrode logic and my hands were shaky as I opened his number and typed out a quick message:

You're an asshole.

And then I hit send and turned my phone off. I stood there staring at it for what felt like hours before I finally left my room and walked into the livingroom. The TV was on, but I couldn't really focus on anything else.

Strolling into the kitchen, I reached into the freezer and pulled out a tub of ice cream, snagging a spoon from the drying rack. I plopped back on the couch and proceeded to snack on spoonfuls right from the tub while I watched some terrible reality show. I ate the whole thing, finishing it off with a few chocolate chips and a mouthful of melted ice cream. By the time I'd cleaned up the dishes, I realized it was three in the morning. I sighed and looked around my apartment. It was so empty.

So lonely.

It took me forever to fall asleep. When I did, my rest was fitful, plagued by nightmares that involved Quinn. I woke up several times throughout the night, and each time I found myself reaching for my phone to check if I had any messages from him, only to remember I had specifically left it turned off.

CHAPTER THIRTY-TWO

Jase

I SLEPT TILL midday, awoken suddenly when I heard someone knocking at the front door. I groaned as I rolled out of bed, running my hands over my face and carding my fingers through my hair. I hoped it wasn't Quinn. I was in no state to deal with him right now. But the person on the other side of the door was one of my neighbors.

"Good afternoon, Jase. I was heading to the food market out of town and wondered if you wanted some of that chili cheese I got you before?" She smiled brightly.

I smiled lightly. Mrs. Jenkins was a sweet old woman who I had bumped into a few times in the local grocery store before she had started to offer to pick up stuff from the farmer's market her son took her to every couple of weeks. "Sure, that'd be great," I said. "Do you want to come in and grab some coffee first?"

She looked shocked but nodded enthusiastically. I led her back inside, and we spent half an hour catching up. Having something other than the previous night to focus on was a blessing, and I immediately felt the weight of the pain

JASE

settle back in my chest as Mrs. Jenkins left to meet her son.

I poured myself another cup of coffee and settled down on the couch to watch some more mindless TV.

By four o'clock, I was bored. I realized I hadn't eaten since breakfast yesterday, so I decided it was time to make myself something to eat. I opened the fridge and stared at the contents for a moment before deciding I had nothing worth eating. Settling for some scrambled eggs and some bacon, I wolfed it down, hardly tasting a bite.

I figured it was about time to turn my phone on and face the music. If Quinn was trying to contact me, there would be a message. But there weren't any texts, only a couple of missed calls.

The one from the station from only

minutes prior caught my attention.

Dialing through to my voicemail, I held the phone to my ear and heard Captain Clarke's voice.

"Jase, are you okay? You haven't checked in all day, and the shift is already underway. Please call me ASAP."

I hung up and put the phone back on its charger.

Fuck.

I had forgotten I had work today. Running my hands through my hair, I glanced at the clock. There was no point going in now. I'd have to make my excuses tomorrow. Moving to place my phone back on the charger, I nearly jumped as it went off in my hand.

Looking at the screen, it showed it was the station. With a tired sigh, I lifted it again and answered. "Yeah?"

JASE

"Jase!" The Captain half yelled. It wasn't angry, just urgent, and I immediately stood straighter. "We need you at the station. There's a huge fire in the central apartment blocks and its spreading fast. Every available unit is being called in. Get to the station and on a truck now!" With that, the line went dead.

What the fuck?

My mind was racing as I ran for the door.

What could have happened so quickly?

Something huge would have to happen to cause a fire like that these days. I didn't bother even tying my shoelaces as I ran out of my apartment and down to the parking lot. I drove like a maniac to get there, not really caring if I got pulled over. I had a valid reason, at least.

CHAPTER THIRTY-THREE

Jase

I PULLED INTO the parking space and raced inside.

"Oh good! You're here. Get in," Carmen called as she tied her boots and shrugged on her protective over-layer. Kicking off my shoes and trousers, I left them in a heap on the floor to save time. I was still fumbling with buttons and ties as

Carmen screeched out of the station, my body sliding in the passenger seat at the speed at which she took corners. The lights and sirens were going, and I could hear others converging toward the same place. We turned onto the main road and roared toward the scene.

It was like something from a movie. The building we approached was completely engulfed in flames. Plumes of black smoke billowed into the air, and embers rained down from above. Police cars blocked off roads leading to the area while fire trucks and ambulances were parked outside. A helicopter hovered overhead.

"Holy shit," I muttered under my breath as the first responders all began arriving. Fire crews were running to their trucks as others arrived at the scene. I saw Carmen's face go pale as she spotted the truck I usually drove in near the front with Mark fighting with the hose that just wouldn't reach any further. She immediately switched lanes and sped toward it, the brakes squealing as she skidded to a stop.

I grabbed my kit bag as she threw herself out the door and rushed over to help.

Mark looked up at us as Carmen dropped to her knees beside him to help him unhook the extra length of hose.

"Carmen! Oh my god," he said as he turned around to look at me.

"Are you all right?" she asked, brushing his hair away from his forehead.

"Yes. Just getting a bit old for this, I guess." He smiled weakly.

I tried to smile but I was too busy

watching the firefighters battle against the flames as they raced upward.

"I'm going in to help!" I called over the noise of the scene and jogged over to the Captain who was directing teams to different points. When he saw me approach, he gave me a grim look.

"This place is coming down fast but there's still people inside. By my count, there's still a kid on the fourth floor who hasn't been brought down or sent for."

I nodded in response. That was where I needed to be.

"On it!" I pulled my oxygen mask from my side and situated it over my face.

"You'll need to hook up your air supply before you go in, Jase," the Captain called out.

I took the regulator and attached it to the tank on my back. Once the tanks were connected, I pulled the straps tight and hooked the mouthpiece into place.

I couldn't believe I was doing this. I hadn't done anything like it since I was in my twenties. My heart started pounding in my chest as I turned away from the Captain and charged at the building.

There was no way I was going to let anyone die.

I ran in through the windows and kept low to the ground as I made my way up the stairs. I was terrified at what I might find waiting for me when I reached the fourth floor. Every thought and prayer in my mind went out to hope that the kid was still okay. I continued my ascent until I finally reached the top of the stairwell.

The smell hit me hard as soon as I opened the door and stepped into the hallway. Flames were shooting out from the third floor and billowing smoke filled the corridor in thick waves. The walls were already starting to melt and there was a heat haze all around. It was almost like the whole floor was on fire.

I sucked in a deep breath and pushed forward, pulling my breathing mask tighter over my face. The air was hot and heavy on my skin, stinging and making my eyes water. I held them closed for a moment, and then opened them and continued to push forward.

When the hallway ended in front of me, I found myself looking down a large open space that led to other rooms beyond.

Where was this kid?

I took another deep breath and moved forward. My eyes started to tear up again but I clenched my jaw and pressed on.

JASE

The flames were growing stronger by the moment as they tore through the ceiling and began to spread out across the floor.

CHAPTER THIRTY-FOUR

Quinn

THE BLAZE THAT swallowed the apartment building in the center of town was worse than anything I had witnessed since that day in New Orleans. It went up so fast, a few seconds at most, and then it burned hot enough to melt metal on the ground below.

The whole block caught fire all at once,

and the flames leaped into the night sky, illuminating the entire city. Flames licked out from every window as though a giant bonfire had been set inside the building.

A column of black smoke rose high above the surrounding buildings, almost reaching the heavens themselves. Whatever had happened to cause this was serious, and the age of the building meant it didn't have the same safety features as the newer ones being built further away from the center.

I shuddered as an eerie sense of déjà vu stole my breath for a moment before I shook my head and pushed it aside. I pushed past the fear and memories choking my throat, determined not to relive the past. This wasn't the same.

I had backed the public up as best as I could to give the other firefighters plenty of space to work with their hoses, but the scale of the fire limited what they could do about the flames. They were forced to douse the building from the outside, and it wasn't long until the roof began to collapse.

"Is everyone out?" Captain Clarke yelled over the roar of the fire. "We're going to have to contain it rather than stop it!"

"Jase is still in there!" Mark called, bundling a small child from around the side of the building and carrying him over to the medical specialists.

"Shit!" The Captain turned his head to his radio to try and contact the man within the building, but my blood had already turned to ice.

Not again.

Images of the New Orleans warehouse

drenched white-hot in flames erupted before my eyes. The scent of burning wood permeated my nose and I swore I could hear the screams of my coworkers from that fateful day.

I couldn't handle it happening again... Not when the last thing that had happened between Jase and I still confused the life out of me. I still didn't understand why he had been so angry. After the evening we had had, I thought that perhaps we had a chance for something real.

This time everyone was getting out alive. I'd make sure of it.

Without much thought or care for the yells of shock and warnings from my colleagues behind me, I flipped my breathing mask down onto my face and ran for the building. My boots slipped and slid on the broken pavement beneath the scorching asphalt, and my hands stung under my gloves from pulling myself through the splintered and melted front entrance with the sheer force of will. But I made it inside.

My heart pounded in my chest as I took in the scene. It was chaos. In the middle of the room, I glanced up through a gaping hole where the ceiling used to be.

Fuck.

What if Jase had fallen through somewhere?

Kicking at the burning debris with my boots, I made sure there was no one beneath it before heading up the stairs. I could hear the Captain over the radio telling me to get my ass back outside, but I refused to even acknowledge him.

"Dude!" Carmen's voice sounded through the radio. "Cap says he was headed to the fourth floor! If you are going to be this level of idiotic, at least you know where not to waste time!" She sounded frustrated and worried. It warmed me a little to know that she understood what would actually help right now. I wasn't coming back out without Jase, so telling me where he was supposed to be was the only thing that could have come over the radio waves that might have just saved my life.

I moved up the stairs two at a time, ignoring the searing pain in my feet and shins as I went. The heat of the flames was so strong I could feel the burn of them through all my protective gear. When I reached the fourth floor, the heat and smell from the fire was so intense I found myself panting heavily through my mask.

"Jase!" I half yelled half coughed. "Jase, can you hear me?"

There was no reply.

He wasn't dead. He had to be alive. I felt sure of it. I pushed through the door and raced toward the end of the corridor.

"Jase, where are you?" I shook my head when I saw the remains of the wall that had collapsed across the hallway.

Fuck.

I was beginning to think this might have been a suicide mission. Then I heard him.

"Fucker!" His voice echoed off the walls. "Get out!"

I climbed over the remains of the wall and kicked open the door on the other side of them. Inside, through the smoke, I could make out a figure on the floor.

"Jase!" I ran through the room and came to a halt next to him. He was struggling with his leg, which had gone through the floor below. There was a great deal of blood and an awful lot of fire surrounding him.

"Fuck!" I said, running forward and trying to lift him up. "Come on." I tried to get him to stand, but his leg was stuck fast. "Goddamn it, man!" I shouted.

The more I struggled to free him, the more obvious it became that he was beyond any help I could give him here.

"Jase," I said, placing my hand on his arm. "Brace yourself." I only had one possibility left, and it was likely going to harm us both. Standing up, I lifted my leg and brought it down heavily on the wooden boards that kept Jase trapped in place. He cried out in pain behind his mask, but the wood splintered. It was so weak from fire, and the water that had been used in the attempt to fight said fire, I had to hope it would give way easily. It was our only shot.

I stomped my foot down on the same spot on the floor a few times before a loud crack sounded around us, and the old floor gave way, dropping us both through to the floor below.

I grabbed Jase tightly as we fell. We landed hard and rolled to our sides, tumbling into a pile. I lost my breath momentarily as Jase's weight pressed down on me and I knew we didn't have time to waste. I knew the entire building would go at any minute.

I quickly pushed him off me and stood up. I searched the room quickly to make sure there was an exit before I leaned down and pulled Jase up, and tossed him over my shoulders. He wasn't going to be able to move quickly enough with that injury. I glanced back at him, gave him a nod, then turned away and ran through the room. He didn't argue, and I couldn't help but wonder if I was carrying Jase's unconscious body.

"I need a medic!" I yelled as soon as we cleared the front entrance.

On the stretcher, Jase was still out of it. They took his helmet off and checked his pulse. His breathing was ragged, but the paramedics were focused on his leg after a new oxygen mask was placed over his face.

"What happened?" Newt, firehouse twenty-one's paramedic asked as he examined the wound.

"He fell through the floor upstairs," I replied.

"All right, we've got it from here. You can meet us at the hospital later." Newt flashed me a knowing look over his shoulder as the two paramedics made their way across the road, and my eyes followed them, watching as they loaded Jase into the ambulance.

I wanted to go with him. I wanted to get into that ambulance and make sure that Jase was okay, but with the fire behind me, I knew I still had a job to do. With a mild curse, I turned and rushed back to the scene to help contain the fire.

CHAPTER THIRTY-FIVE

Quinn

IT TOOK HOURS to control the flames, and by the time we did, there was little more to the apartment than a charred shell.

Most firefighters went home exhausted at the end, but our team and Captain Clarke all ended up trudging to the hospital to find out how Jase was. He was stable, and we were told his lungs would be fine, but his leg would take a lot of physiotherapy before he would be able to work again.

"It will take a lot of effort from him." The doctor sighed.

"He'll do it. He's stubborn enough," Mark commented, a rippling of agreement sounding from the rest of us.

Not wanting to bother the doctors any more than they already were, everyone decided to leave and come back during visiting hours the following day.

At least, everyone else did.

I mumbled an excuse that I needed to visit the restroom so I would see them at work the following day, but I did not leave the hospital. I couldn't. I needed to know that Jase was okay. I needed to see him when he was conscious, to make sure he knew that everyone was there for him through the therapy he would need. I needed... Oh, I don't know what I needed. I just needed to see him.

The images of him surrounded by fire played in my head over and over.

What if I had been slower?

What if I had listened to the Captain and not gone back inside?

The idea of losing Jase from my life made me feel physically sick to my stomach, and twice I did have to visit the restroom to unload my stomach.

Once I felt better, I found myself wandering around the hospital corridors aimlessly until I finally saw him. His face was pale and bloodless, his eyes wide and terrified, and his hair matted with sweat. They wouldn't let me talk to him yet, though. The nurse said he was being taken into surgery to fix his leg and someone would let me know when he was in recovery.

I took to pacing in the waiting room and about an hour in, I recognized Jase's parents as they finally arrived at the hospital. It looked like Jase's father had literally run across the city, and now he was striding up the corridor like a man on a mission, his wife half running beside him. They were older than I remembered them, but I recognized them instantly. Jase shared so many of their features.

"Mr. and Mrs. Turner," I called, jogging over to them.

"Sorry, we're in a rush."

"Jase is still in surgery," I called after them, watching as they came to a stop and turned back to face me. "They are making sure his leg is as clean as possible, so recovery is easiest. I paid the bill in advance. I just wanted him to have the best chance at getting back to work."

Mr. Turner's eyes narrowed at me. He was a beefy man with a mustache adorning his upper lip and a receding hairline. He had a nose that stuck out slightly too far, which only served to give him an even more intimidating look. His wife, on the other hand, looked like she was about to burst into tears at any second. She was petite and pretty, with dark brown hair that fell down her back in ringlets. Her eyes were sad and puffy, and I could tell she was afraid. Mr. Turner moved forward then, stepping between her and me.

"And who exactly are you?"

"Quinn Sanders, sir. I work with Jase." I glanced from Mr. Turner to his wife, who looked at me with a slight curiosity in her sad eyes.

"Sanders? The preacher's son?"

"Yes, sir."

"Hmm." He hummed in deliberation before sighing. "Well, thank you. It's nice to see a member of that family actually helping out someone else."

I chuckled darkly. "Yes, well, my father and I see things very differently."

He smiled grimly at me as if he knew exactly what I was referring to. The knowledge of my sexuality, despite my upbringing, was probably a rumor that had spread far by now. "Yes, I imagine you do. Now, I must find a doctor to find out what's happening."

His wife gave me a look that said 'thank you' as they turned and hurried away. I smiled softly back at her, deciding to give them space and venture to the cafeteria for some coffee. There was no chance I was sleeping tonight until I knew Jase was awake and okay.

CHAPTER THIRTY-SIX

Quinn

WHEN I RETURNED to the floor where Jase was being treated, I saw a familiar figure sitting outside his room. Captain Clarke was leaning against the wall, looking tired and drawn. I sat next to him, sipping at my cup of instant coffee. "I thought you went home," I commented. "How are you doing?"

He laughed bitterly. "Like shit. I'm used to seeing people injured, but this time it was one of mine, and I've never seen anyone's leg torn up so badly."

"You're allowed to be angry. I know you care about him a lot."

He shook his head. "No, no. I know that. Just... I keep going over what happened in my mind. I can't believe I almost stopped you from going in for him." He took a deep breath before continuing. "I'm sorry, Quinn. I really am."

It was my turn to laugh, albeit weakly. "Don't apologize to me. You did nothing wrong, Cap. You were following the guidelines, and there was every chance me going in there would have killed me too."

"Maybe. But I should have trusted you.

I should have trusted your instincts. I just..." He sighed and rubbed his face. "This has been the worst day of my career."

I felt for him, and with a hand on his shoulder, I squeezed slightly. "At least he is alive, and he will be fine."

Captain Clarke nodded but didn't say anything. We sat quietly for a while, drinking our coffees in companionable silence.

CHAPTER THIRTY-SEVEN

Jase

I WOKE UP from dreams of fire, brimstone, smoke, and ash. The smell was still heavy in my nose, and the taste was on my tongue. There were no birds, no animals, nothing alive that I could see. It looked like the world had been destroyed by some terrible natural disaster. The ceiling I focused on as I drifted back to the world of the waking was a dingy off-white, and I recognized the rhythmic beeping of a hospital. I tried to sit up, but pain shot through my head, and my stomach clenched with nausea.

"Shit," I grunted and fell back onto the bed.

"Easy!" A nurse was hovering over me, pulling out an IV drip and peering at the readout. She tapped something into a small computer pad and then turned back to me. "You're awake, good."

I nodded. My memory was fuzzy; I couldn't remember very much about what had happened or where we had ended up. "Where am I?"

She smiled. "The doctor will be down soon to talk to you. He's just finishing up another case."

As she walked away, I noticed her

name badge said 'Lisa'. I closed my eyes again, trying to get more rest before the doc came. After a few minutes, the door opened, and a man in a lab coat entered. He glanced at me briefly, then moved around the bed, examining me. "Well, looks like you've come through all right this time. You got pretty banged up, though. How do you feel?"

I grimaced, feeling the dull aches in my body, trying not to move too much. "I feel okay?"

"Well, that could be the drugs," the doctor admitted. "I'm just going to check on your leg, then get the nurse to redress it. After that, you have visitors." He patted my shoulder. "Try and stay awake for them."

I nodded. I didn't want to sleep anymore anyway. After a minute, the nurse returned and began unwrapping the dressing. My eyes widened as I saw the stitched-up wound on my shin. I remembered the pain of falling through the floorboards as they splintered and ripped and dug into my leg. I winced as she pulled the gauze clear of the gash.

"That looks painful," she said, cleaning it with antiseptic soap and bandaging me again.

"I suspect that it would be if I wasn't on the meds," I mumbled.

"But it's looking good. No signs of infection." The doctor smiled. "I'll check on it again tomorrow."

With it all dressed again, they left me alone in the room. I watched the door as it closed, blocking out the multitude of hospital sounds. I sighed and lay back, feeling drained, waiting for my visitors to come.

After a little while, I heard footsteps and saw the door to the room open. I sat up, keeping my legs tucked under the blankets, as my parents walked in. My mother quickly launched herself across the room to hug me, pressing kisses to my forehead and mumbling over and over how glad she was that I was okay. It made me smile.

My father stepped back and looked me over carefully. "You look better now. God knows how you survived that fire."

"Now?" I asked. "How long have I been here?"

"Three days," my father said, taking a seat in the chair beside my bed. I rubbed my face with my hand, and I realized just how much my beard had grown in that time. I could remember the heat of the flames surrounding me, the feeling of not being able to get myself out of that hole, the fiery pain from my leg, and the sinking feeling in my stomach that I was going to die there.

And Quinn.

I remembered him appearing just as I was starting to give up.

Glancing from my parents to the door, I wondered if I had imagined it. He wouldn't have been stupid enough to come looking for me in a fire like that.

But if he didn't, then how did I get out?

"He had to go home for a shower," my mother said with a smile as she noticed my gaze hovering on the door. I glanced at her with a raised eyebrow.

"Quinn. He's a lovely young man, but he was starting to smell quite badly, having not washed after the fire for three days."

"He was here?"

"For all three days, yes," my father grumbled. "I'll admit, if you have to be gay, you could do worse than him."

My face flushed immediately, and I shifted uncomfortably, which made my leg twinge in pain. "You know?" I braced myself for a lecture or worse, but the man merely rolled his eyes.

"Your mother told me. And frankly, I'll take you gay and alive over straight and dead if that man loving you was what saved your life." He crossed his arms over his chest, obviously not one hundred percent comfortable with the idea, but still, as an old-school Texan, I wasn't sure I could have ever wished for better.

"He doesn't love me," I grumbled,

remembering the man he lived with.

To my surprise, my father barked out a laugh. "Oh, please. There are only two people I'd run into a fire for, and that's you and your mother, let alone a building that is literally falling in on itself because of those flames."

"We're firefighters, Dad. It's what we do." I sighed.

"Your Captain said he ignored direct orders not to enter that building because it was so bad."

"And we are so grateful he did," my mother added, reaching over to take my hand and squeeze it. When they put it like that, it did make me feel a sliver of hope. Surely it said something if Quinn had been the one to ignore orders and run in when even my long-term colleagues Mark and Johnson hadn't.

JASE

Still, even if he didn't, I knew my father was accepting of my lifestyle now as well. The weight lifted from my shoulders by that very idea made me feel exhausted to my core. Or perhaps it was the drugs.

CHAPTER THIRTY-EIGHT

Jase

I SPENT THE next few days in and out of sleep. The pain meds and anti-nausea injection they gave me a few times a day so I could eat made me feel as though the world was spinning, like I'd had a hundred drinks too many before I fell asleep again. Every time I was awake, I seemed to have missed Quinn. But according to the nurses, I was only allowed a couple of visitors at a time, and when my parents were there, he would step aside and wait down in the cafeteria. Apparently, he had practically been camping out there, and every time a nurse who knew my situation went down, they gave him an update.

I wanted to see him so badly, but it was a week after my surgery that they finally allowed me out of my room with strict instructions not to put any unwarranted pressure on my leg.

Eager to see him, I managed to get myself into a wheelchair and then rolled through the halls and down to the cafeteria. It didn't take me long to spot him.

He had his back to the door, which meant he hadn't seen me yet. He was bent over the table with one hand propping his head up while the other absently stirred the coffee in front of him.

Carefully weaving my way through the tables over to him, I noticed dark rings around his eyes and that his hair was still damp from a recent shower, one he had likely rushed if his unshaven appearance was anything to go by.

I stopped by his elbow with a sigh. I'd missed his face more than I was willing to admit.

His arm twitched as he felt me there. He turned to face me and his eyes widened comically before he grinned. "Jase," he exclaimed. "Hi! Erm... Are you okay? How is your leg?" He fumbled a little with his coffee as he half-rose in his seat, not knowing whether to embrace me or not.

"It's fine," I answered, giving him an apologetic shrug of my shoulders. "The doctor said you didn't get too hurt coming into get me. That true?"

Quinn smiled softly, his eyes full of a soft emotion that made me melt. "Twisted ankle, nothing that I couldn't walk off." He chuckled. "I'm just glad I could be here for you. The medical staff said you'd probably need someone to help you out when you were up and mobile again."

I positioned my chair up against the table, and Quinn continued. "I know your parents will help, but I just want to say that I will too, if you need anything."

I tilted my head to the side as I watched him. "Why?"

He looked at me with confusion clear on his features.

"Why are you going so far for me?" I

asked.

Quinn laughed bitterly. "Oh, come on, surely you know why?"

"No, I don't," I replied. "One minute, I might think you like me, then I find that you live with your partner."

"What partner?"

"Don't mess with me, Quinn," I muttered irritably. "I saw you kissing him in public. I can't believe you slept with me in the same place he lives."

Quinn flushed slightly, and his cheeks grew redder as he took a deep breath, realizing what I had seen and what I was talking about. I expected some kind of defense, but instead, I was met with a mildly hysterical laugh from him as he hung his head.

"God, what a clusterfuck of a misunderstanding," he mumbled before turning his beautiful eyes to look me directly in the face. "There's nothing between Jared and me. He's got a long-term girlfriend he's planning on proposing to."

"But, I saw..."

"Me kiss him. Right. Which means you saw a guy from my parents' church giving me grief too, right?"

I nodded slowly.

"Well, he was giving me crap about rumors of me being gay and telling me he knew I'd never do something so disgusting and all that shit. So I kissed Jared to prove a point and make him fuck off."

Thinking back to the view I had seen, it had made sense. Quinn had looked very uncomfortable with whatever had been said to him, and the man had quickly stormed off when Quinn had kissed his friend.

"So there's nothing going on with him?" I questioned carefully.

Quinn shook his head vehemently. "Nothing. We're friends like we always have been, but there's no more to it than that."

"Oh..." I whispered.

"Is that why you left so angrily the other night?" Quinn asked. "You thought I'd cheated on him with you?"

Heat spread over my cheeks as I looked away from him in embarrassment. "Kinda," I admitted. "And that I thought maybe there was something between us, but suddenly I just felt like a bit of fun for you."

Quinn looked horrified. "Absolutely not. I don't think you were even 'just a bit of fun' back in Lafayette. I was gutted when I woke up, and you were gone."

I looked around in surprise. "Really?"

"Yeah." He smiled.

"I was so scared about how good it had been and that my secret would be out for good."

"I promised I wouldn't out you..."

"I know..."

Silence fell between us. I didn't know what that conversation meant. From the way Quinn sipped his coffee, I could tell he wasn't sure what to do or say anymore either.

Slowly, with a lot of courage, probably from the drugs in my system, I reached over and linked my fingers with his. His hand was warm and strong, and I immediately remembered how they had held me steady while he broke the floorboards to free me. I remembered how he pulled me close to keep me from further harm as we fell through the floor, and I remembered how he had grunted a little as he threw me over his shoulder right before I passed out.

"You saved my life," I whispered.

"I couldn't bear to let you die," he whispered back. "When you passed out, I thought I'd lost you. I couldn't do anything else in there, so I just pushed it all aside and focused on getting you out safely."

I swallowed hard, looking up at him. "Thank you." At that moment, my father's words rang in my head, 'Better gay and alive,' and I reached forward to take hold of Quinn's chin, holding him still as I leaned across the table to kiss him.

He let out a sound of surprise, which was honestly adorable, before he kissed me back eagerly. After a moment, he pulled back.

"You do realize this is public, right?" He chuckled.

"Yeah, I know." I could feel myself flush a little when it was pointed out. "But I could have died. All of a sudden, being out as gay doesn't seem so scary."

Quinn looked at me for a long moment, then said, "I'm glad you're safe."

The sincerity of those words made something inside me flutter, and I felt like I needed to say something more. "I'm glad you are too." There was silence again as we finished our food. When we were done, I wiped the crumbs from my lips, and put my napkin down on the table. "Thank you, Quinn."

"Don't mention it," he replied. "Though, if you want to thank me; you'll let me take you on a date when you get out of here." He flashed me a grin.

"Actually, I was hoping you'd come and stay with me for a bit... you know, make sure I don't strain my leg around my apartment." I raised an eyebrow, knowing he had already offered to help once but amused at the surprise on his face nonetheless.

"I can absolutely do that," he promised, flashing me a megawatt smile and leaning across the table to kiss me once more.

CHAPTER THIRTY-NINE

Quinn

I MADE GOOD on my promise when Jase was let out of the hospital to return home. His parents had wanted him to move in with them for a while, but he was adamant that he would be fine in his apartment because I would be there to help him. I honestly wasn't sure if his father was going to be okay with that, the man hadn't been the most friendly toward me whenever I had seen him in the hospital, but Jase told me that was just what he was like. A surly old Texan who didn't really like to show too many emotions. The fact he had shaken my hand and told me that if I didn't treat Jase well, he would shoot me in the face with a shotgun was apparently a good sign.

The drive back to Jase's place took about an hour due to traffic, and taking it easy since I didn't want to aggravate Jase's leg. Once we arrived at his building, I climbed out and got Jase settled in a wheelchair on the sidewalk, then parked the car down the street and walked back over to the front door. It was now dark outside, so I couldn't see much of anything, but when I reached the door,

JASE

I could hear some sort of commotion inside.

"Welcome home," came a yell as I opened the door to his apartment. "Glad you're here! We were beginning to think you weren't coming."

Jase looked up from where he was sitting in his wheelchair to find the rest of the crew from the station waiting inside. He glanced up at me, and I gave a half shoulder roll shrug. Of course, I had known this greeting would be waiting for him, but I hadn't wanted to spoil anything.

He wheeled himself over to the group and flashed me a smile before turning back to them.

"What's all the fuss," he asked as he maneuvered himself into the middle of the room. "It's not like I nearly died or anything." He smirked and chuckled as Mark reached over to smack his head lightly before hugging him.

"Yeah, yeah," Mark said as he stepped away from him. "But you *did* almost die, my friend. But that's not why we are here."

"Huh," Jase asked.

"We saw you snogging Quinn at the hospital," Johnson laughed. "We wanted to make sure you knew we were all cool with it, and you didn't have to worry about telling us." Jase spluttered at the bluntness of the message, his cheeks turning a shade of red that I was starting to adore.

"And by the way," Gage added. "We all agree you're the hottest between you two, even though you can't walk right now." That got another laugh out of everyone except Jase, who gave him a look like he had lost his mind.

"Well, I can agree with that." I laughed.

"Gross." Carmen laughed from the sofa. "No sappy shit on shift, though, all right? I like keeping my food in my stomach," she teased. It was such a light atmosphere, and the way they had addressed the news of Jase being gay was almost like they weren't taking it seriously, or really didn't care one way or the other. But I could see from the relief and the smile on Jase's face that this was the best way for him to be received. His sexuality would change absolutely nothing about his relationships with his coworkers. They were still teasing and laughing with him, which was most likely exactly what he'd feared losing.

"That's actually the second thing we

wanted to talk to you about," Johnson said after giving Jase a quick glance that was mildly serious. "We have a bet going at how long it'll take you to be back on your feet, and if I don't win, I'm going to put you back in that chair." His face changed to a cheeky grin as Jase rolled his eyes and reached out to swat his friend's arm.

"Don't go betting on my injuries!" He laughed. "I'm already feeling better than I have been all week, so I say I'll be walking again within a week."

"A week?" Johnson repeated. "That's pretty optimistic."

"Damn straight, but you know me." Jase flashed him a cocky grin.

I just shook my head, a smile gracing my lips at my stubborn man.

CHAPTER FORTY

Quinn

THE BANTER AND laughter went on for a couple of hours before the visitors decided they should probably head off as they all had to work the next day. I had already booked the time off to ensure Jase was supported when needed. Once silence fell through the apartment, Jase looked up at me with a raised eyebrow. "You knew they'd seen us?"

"Of course." I smiled. "They all gave me a similar speech to one that your dad did. If I hurt you, they'll make sure I get stuck in the next fire-filled building." He blushed slightly at the protectiveness of so many around him. "I told them that if I have hurt you, I'll walk into that building myself," I assured him, stepping over to him and leaning down to catch his lips with mine. This kiss differed from our first one. He held onto my waist and pulled me close, and a soft moan escaped his mouth.

After a few moments, I felt him loosen his grip and then pull back to look into my eyes. "I want to explore more with you," Jase whispered. "Not just tonight, but whenever we can. I want to feel you against me. I want to know every inch of your body." He traced a finger along my jawline before I heard him chuckle.

My heart thudded heavily as I nodded slowly, stepping toward the bedroom. Jase wheeled himself in there first, but the door didn't even close before I strode over to him, pinned him into the chair, and crushed my mouth against his. I moved my hands down his arms and across his chest before reaching up to grab his hair and pull his head back, deepening the kiss.

His fingers wrapped around my wrists, and he pushed my hair away from my face with his other hand while I continued to suckle on his tongue and nip at his bottom lip.

"Fuck," Jase gasped as I broke away.

"That's the idea..." I purred, slipping my arms under his legs and lifting him enough to move him from the chair to the bed, where I crowded him against the mattress.

"God, I love you," he breathed.

I stopped for a moment, pulling back and gazing down into his eyes as the words echoed in my ears. They were genuine and honest, full of emotion I could see clearly in his features.

"I love you too," I replied, pressing my mouth against his again.

This time, Jase wrapped his arms around my torso and held me tight as I explored every inch of his mouth with my tongue. When I slipped my hands inside his shirt and cupped his hard, firm chest, I felt his hands glide down my sides and grab hold of my hips. I moaned softly against his lips when he thrust his tongue into my mouth, swirling it around mine before pulling away. He attempted to shift his leg and hissed slightly in pain.

"Fuck." Jase groaned.

"You shouldn't move," I whispered. "Leave this to me."

He nodded, letting go of me and allowing me to remove his shirt. I tossed it aside and began unbuttoning his pants, pushing them and his underwear past his knees, making sure to be careful of his injury. I watched him from under lowered lashes as the head of his cock sprung upward, wet and glistening with his arousal. I ran my hands between his thighs and then around his ass, squeezing gently. He shivered at the touch, and I chuckled.

"I think you like being touched," I said between kisses as I made my way down over his belly, my tongue teasing his furry treasure trail downward.

His gaze flashed up to meet mine, and he nodded slightly. "I do..."

I leaned down and licked along the length of Jase's shaft, tasting the salty pearl of fluid that leaked from the tip. I swirled my tongue around the head, lapping up the precum before pressing my lips against his skin. A low, guttural sound escaped his throat as I slid my lips along the length of him, teasing him with my tongue. I picked up the pace, taking him halfway into my mouth and then pulling back, working him rapidly with my mouth. He was moaning and panting by the time I took his entire length into my mouth, letting it bump against the back of my throat before once again pulling upward and hollowing my cheeks, sucking hard on the last inch or two.

I pulled back from him with an audible pop and sat upright, looking up at him with lust-filled eyes. "Do you want to fuck me?" I asked softly.

"Yes," Jase hissed. "Please."

Pulling my clothes from my body quickly, I crawled onto the bed and straddled his lap, watching as he blindly reached to the side of the bed and fumbled with a small box. As he pulled it open, I smirked as I saw lube and condoms. "I knew you weren't going to be shy about this," I teased.

"I'm not," he growled. "And neither are you... right?"

I laughed softly, running my fingers across his cheekbone and down the column of his neck. "Right."

"Let me touch you," Jase urged, his voice husky.

I obliged, keeping my weight off his thighs as he sat up beneath me and spread lube over his fingers. His teeth nipped and bit at my chest, leaving small marks behind as his first finger invaded my body from below. I groaned deeply as the digit moved inside me, exploring me in a way no one had ever done before. I had never been the one on the receiving end, but as he touched me, I couldn't help but burn for him. I wanted everything I could get from Jase, and the idea of riding him and watching his pleasure made me hotter by the second.

"Fucking hell." He sighed, and I felt his fingers leave my body as he worked the condom onto his dick. He eased himself into position, and I lifted myself from the bed, taking care to avoid jarring his leg. I moved closer to him and reached for his hand, threading our fingers together as I positioned myself above him.

Jase looked up at me with wide eyes, and I smiled as I lowered myself onto his hard erection. The sensation was incredible. It was a tight fit, and I wiggled against his body, enjoying the feeling of his hardness and warmth.

I placed my hands on his shoulders and leaned down, kissing him once more. Then I slowly started to move, rocking my hips back and forth as I impaled myself upon him, the initial burning stretch turning quickly into an unbelievable feeling of fullness.

"Oh god..." Jase groaned, his head falling back onto the pillow.

I rocked slowly, feeling his hands slide down my waist and grip my hips as he tried to pull me closer to him. There was a slight pain that accompanied my movements, but his hands on my hips kept me from speeding up while I got used to his size.

I felt my muscles tense as he hit my deepest parts, brushing again and again over my sweet spot, and I sighed in relief when there was nothing but mind-boggling pleasure left in my body. I felt him tighten beneath me, and I leaned down further to kiss him again. He tasted like salt, and I smacked my lips against his, unable to stop myself from biting his lower lip. I reached up and grabbed handfuls of his hair, holding his face still so I could devour him as much as possible.

My body was on fire, and I needed more. I rocked harder, increasing the pace. Soon, I was slamming my hips against his, feeling his hands dig into my hips as he forced himself not to thrust up to meet me in case it strained his leg. I didn't mind. I could feel every movement of his body as his breathing became labored, and his voice grew louder with each passing second. I leaned down and buried my face against his shoulder, unable to take any more.

"Fuck. Jase, you feel so good inside me," I groaned against his skin.

He held my hips tightly in his grasp while he kissed the side of my neck. "You're so tight, baby," he growled.

I moaned at the sound of his husky voice, digging my nails into his shoulders as I continued to ride him. My body was ready to come. I wanted to let go and scream my release. But I wanted Jase to come first. I needed to see him lose control. I needed to hear him say my name while we both came undone.

I slid my hands down his strong arms, moving my hand between us until I found the base of his cock, stroking him hard and fast even as I rode him. I was almost there. I could feel it building inside me. His breath was ragged, and I could tell he was close too. I gripped his thighs tighter, holding him firmly in place as I felt the pressure of his swelling cock build within me, pressing against the walls of my body, as my own balls pulled up tight and heat coiled in my belly.

I dug my nails into his thighs as I cried out, my back arching, feeling my orgasm take me over completely. I watched as Jase stiffened beneath me as my body clamped around him and sent him over the edge as well. I felt his body tense as his release caused him to jerk beneath me.

Slowly, I began to rock my hips, milking every last bit that he had for me before I finally stilled my hips and leaned forward to capture his lips again. The kiss we shared was slower, sensual, and loving. Heavy breathing merged together between the kisses, and for a while, we just stayed there, enjoying the aftermath and losing ourselves in the emotions that filled the kisses.

We were quiet for long enough before I pulled away and slid off him, lying alongside Jase. We lay side-by-side, and I wrapped an arm around him, pulling him into me as I snuggled him against my chest.

"I love you so much, Jase," I whispered.

His fingers traced circles along my arm as he turned onto his side to look up at me. "I love you too, baby."

For a moment, time stood still. We simply stared at one another, understanding what had just happened. I knew I loved him, but this was different. This was more than I'd ever thought it would be. Jase had shown me everything I hadn't known about myself. And now I understood just how deep my feelings ran for him.

Jase pulled me closer, kissing me softly as he rested his hand on the back of my head. The warmth of his body seeped through my skin, and a smile touched his lips when I pressed mine to him in return.

He pulled away from me then, looking up at me with those bright eyes that seemed like they could see right inside me. He brushed a strand of hair behind my ear, then leaned over to kiss my neck, making me shiver underneath him. My heart began beating faster, and my breath quickened. His hands moved down my sides, slipping between us to explore my abdomen and toy with the dark trail of hair there.

"I'm not a young man anymore," I warned him. "But if you keep roaming, I'm going to want to do you again soon enough."

Jase smirked a little. "Is that a promise? Because I could really do with the feeling of you inside me as well."

I raised an eyebrow, shifting so I could roll him onto his back and place my arms on either side of his head to box him in.

"Oh really? You think you're up to

that? What about your leg."

He nodded. "To hell with my leg."

"And here I was trying to be nice." I chuckled. There was something about Jase that made me feel like an excited teenager again. I could feel the blood in my body running south in an attempt to have more as soon as possible.

"I want the night we should have had if I hadn't misunderstood," Jase grumbled, reaching up to bury his fingers in my hair and pull me down for another hungry kiss.

My entire body trembled as our tongues tangled together. I felt my control slipping by the second, and I wanted nothing more than to lose myself inside him. It wasn't just the sex, though. I'd never been with anyone who was so open and honest with me. He showed me things I didn't know existed within myself. But more importantly, he showed me how much I truly cared about him. How much I needed him.

I reached down and grasped his cock beneath the sheets, stroking him slowly until he moaned and rolled his hips against my touch, growing half-hard already. Jase growled low in his throat, rolling his hips more forcefully.

"You're killing me," he groaned, and I laughed, knowing exactly how he felt.

I sat up and pushed his legs further apart, so I could see his bare ass and the thick length of his shaft standing proudly from between his legs. I loved the way he looked.

"Spread your knees, baby," I ordered, and he complied immediately. He moved carefully with his injured leg, and I propped a pillow beneath it so he could rest it in that position easier.

I dropped my mouth to his balls, licking and sucking them gently before I teased his opening with my tongue until it softened and fluttered under my ministrations. Jase let out a deep moan, and I could feel my own length hardening by the second.

"Fuck," Jase swore, his voice rough and strained as I licked the underside of his shaft. I nipped his sac with my teeth and sucked on his ball sack, enjoying the way he bucked against my face. I worked my way up the base of his cock, licking and sucking along the way until I got to the tip. I swirled my tongue around the slit, coating it in my saliva, then wrapped my fist around his base and stroked him up and down a few times.

"Mmm, you taste good," I murmured.

"I need you inside me, now," he demanded.

I grinned, slicking up my fingers before pushing a finger through the tight ring of muscle past his entrance and sliding it in and out, watching his stomach muscles tense and relax as I did. I loved the way he tasted as I kissed along his hips, the musky scent of his skin.

I slipped two fingers into him now, thrusting them in and out. He clenched tight around them, and I added a third, moving them in and out of him with slow, deliberate strokes. He was so fucking hot and wet. Every inch of him was slick with his arousal.

"Shit, you are so fucking gorgeous," I hissed as I pulled my fingers from him and surged up to slam my lips against his. Lifting his healthy leg up onto my shoulder, I pressed the tip of my cock to his hole and paused, smirking into the kiss as he whined and attempted to push down onto me. Pulling away from his lips briefly, I ran my tongue along his jawline. "You want me that badly?" I whispered.

"Yes," Jase panted. "Come on. Fuck me."

I smiled, pulling my hand from his hip and grabbing a condom from the bedside table. I tore it open with my teeth, rolling the latex over my hard, throbbing cock in one smooth movement. I gripped his hips tightly, lifting him off the bed slightly so I could drive into him. His legs were still spread wide, and I moved my hand to hold his thigh against my chest, keeping him steady as I slid to the hilt with a single thrust.

JASE

"Ahhh," Jase let out a long breath, tilting his head back. "God, yes."

I held him in place with one arm wrapped around his waist while I pumped my hips, working my length in and out of him with slow, easy thrusts. I leaned forward and brushed my nose against his neck, inhaling the warm scent of him. He was so fucking sexy and delicious. I couldn't get enough of him.

His breathing grew heavier as I began to move faster, pounding his ass roughly with each thrust. I bit down on his shoulder, and he let out a throaty groan.

"More," he begged.

I chuckled, biting down a little harder, making the most of the moment and creating a mark that would surely last for days. The feeling of possession ran through me as I pulled back to inspect my work.

"Mine," I growled a little, shifting my hips to piston against the sensitive bundle of nerves within Jase that made his back arch and his mouth fall open in silent moans of pure pleasure.

He was mine. And I was his.

CHAPTER FORTY-ONE

Jase

THE FOLLOWING DAY, we slept late, waking up only when the sun had begun to rise. We showered together, thoroughly washing each other's hair and bodies but avoiding anything more intimate. I was stuck in a shower chair for some of it. For other parts, Quinn held my body close to him to support my weight so we could share kisses and feel the heat of each other's bodies close. When we were both clean, he helped me out into the livingroom, where we sat on the couch and watched television.

He had left his phone charging on the coffee table while we were asleep, and he didn't seem worried about it that morning either. It was bliss to lose yourself in the company of someone, and I still couldn't believe he had actually said he loved me. Even though I'd never been one to be romantic or emotional, there was something special about being with him, knowing that he wanted me.

Even better was the fact that my parents and my coworkers knew about my sexuality and hadn't cared.

Over the next few weeks, my father often came over to take me to the clinic at the hospital where my physical therapy would be held. He was retired and knew that Quinn needed to return to work, so he had been the first to offer to take me to my appointments. Each time, my mother stayed at my apartment to clean and cook so Quinn did not have too much to do after a twelve-hour shift.

Quinn was sweet and understanding, and even though he was always tired from working nights, he tried to help as much as possible. He went grocery shopping for us, made sure I ate right, and cooked meals for me every night. The only downside was that I no longer had access to the gym or any of the machines. Still, I got plenty of exercise with the routines my PT, Frankie, provided. And my appointments were easy to manage.

"Look, Jase..." my father said on the

first day I was given a crutch to use instead of a wheelchair.

I glanced over at him where he had stopped before getting in the car. He looked uncomfortable.

"I just wanted to say... I'm so fucking proud of you."

My eyebrows shot up at the genuine softness in the old man's voice. "That's really nice, Dad," I replied, reaching across the car to squeeze his hand.

He squeezed mine back, smiling. "But look, this whole thing isn't exactly easy for me."

I knew he meant the sexuality thing, but I stayed quiet.

"I mean, yeah, it makes sense. You're a good guy. But it still feels weird..." he trailed off.

I sighed and rubbed my forehead. He

was so nervous about things like this. I thought it was because he was afraid of what people might think of him or his family. My father wasn't very religious, but he was still raised in a very different era. He expected certain behavior from those who lived in our town. He had grown up in an area where it was illegal to see two men holding hands or kissing in public and where gay marriage was never going to be accepted.

"It's okay, Dad," I started, but he raised a hand to cut me off.

"No, let me say this, okay?" He sucked in a deep breath and looked down at his shoes. "I love your boyfriend," he admitted, looking up at me again. "I know he's not my son, but he's doing everything right by you, and if it weren't for him, I don't know... I definitely couldn't have afforded your surgeries. He's a good man, and I'm just glad you have someone who cares so much for you."

I smiled at the compliment. "Thanks," I told him. "And that's all I need to hear. I just never wanted to lose you and Mom."

"Idiot. You'll never lose us." He flashed me a smile. "You're my boy."

After that, I did a lot of thinking about my father. I realized how lucky I was to have grown up in such a loving home and how I should be grateful to have had the upbringing I did. It also made me think about Quinn and the way his parents hadn't spoken to him once since he came out publicly. He never spoke about it, but there must have been pain deep within him, knowing that his parents couldn't love him enough to get past something that their religion condemned. Their actions were a sign of their lack of understanding and acceptance. They just didn't understand that they needed to change, not Quinn.

I thought back on all the times that I'd read about someone who was persecuted because of being gay. The stories always left me feeling sad and scared. Once more, I was struck by the level of courage Quinn had despite the actions he had performed in his youth due to fear. If only other people could find the same strength in themselves, then maybe things would start to change for everyone.

CHAPTER FORTY-TWO

Jase

THE NEXT DAY while Quinn was at work, I caught myself staring into space as I stared at the TV screen. Something was bothering me. As I sat there waiting for Quinn to come home from work, I tried to figure out what it was. After a few minutes, it hit me like a ton of bricks—I felt guilty.

Since being together, Quinn had been so affectionate, working hard to fix any remaining wounds I might still have from his actions at school, but I had not once acknowledged his pain in return. I knew that Quinn's family had hurt him deeply, especially when he was young, but I didn't want our relationship to be built off one-sided guilt from the past.

"You all right?" Quinn asked as he walked through the door with a smile on his face. He was such a beautiful man who had changed so much from his youth. His skin was now smooth and clear, without a single blemish or scar. Those eyes of his were now the most expressive part of him. Whenever he looked at me, I felt as though we were the only two souls in the world.

With a small smile, I took hold of my

crutch and used it to get to my feet, hobbling over to where he had unpacked his backpack in the kitchen.

"Getting better every day." I flashed him a megawatt smile.

He laughed softly as he shook his head, then held out something to me. "I picked you up a treat," he said.

As I looked at the object in his hand, I smiled lightly. It was a specific brand of non-alcoholic beer, which I enjoyed but couldn't get at the local shop. Being on the medications that I was, I couldn't drink anything with alcohol content, and it had been something I missed. Even after a long shift, he still thought about me and expressed it in small but meaningful actions.

"Thank you," I said softly as he placed the can on the counter and then wrapped an arm around my waist, pulling me close to him.

"Are you sure you are okay," he asked.

"Yeah. I was just thinking about you," I admitted. "I want to say I forgive you for everything from when we were younger. You are an amazing person and so brave for coming out the other side of that fear instilled in you by the church."

Quinn tilted his head to the side as I spoke, his eyes glistening a little with emotion. "That's why I love you. You always see the good in people, despite what they do. I'm happy that you feel like I have changed for the better. I would never be able to forgive myself if I hadn't." He chuckled. "Although, there is one thing I can't forgive myself for."

He glanced down and took hold of my hand, lifting it up and pressing his lips to the faded scar that lingered on my wrist from that awful night I had chickened out of ending everything.

"I will spend the rest of my life making sure you never feel that bad ever again, and I'll never forgive myself for being a factor in that decision, in making you feel the way you did."

It was true. Since he had been living here with me, Quinn had made me happier than anyone else alive. The pain I had lived with was finally beginning to fade away. We were both free men now, and neither of us was going back.

I kissed him gently before reaching over and snagging the beer can off the counter. I opened it up and took a sip. "I'll hold you to that." I smiled, liking his promise to be around for the foreseeable future. I had no idea how the future would turn out, but knowing I wouldn't be alone was nice.

With a soft kiss to my forehead, Quinn carried his things into the bedroom, and I watched him go, feeling a sense of pride in myself for having managed to live this long. I had left the past behind, and even if I was now facing a few months of therapy, I had grown stronger in so many ways, and I had someone by my side.

Life was changing, and I was starting to accept that it really could change for the better.

EPILOGUE

Jase

IT DIDN'T TAKE long for Quinn to move in with me permanently. I had a bed that was big enough for the both of us, so I offered it up, and he accepted without hesitation.

Of course, there were some moments when I felt like we were moving too fast, but those times passed quickly as well.

We would spend hours talking about our favorite things or just sitting around watching TV while occasionally playing video games together.

Being open about who I was allowed me to deepen the friendships I had with my coworkers too, and my social life expanded as a result. Johnson and Carmen had ended up getting together and took to joining me for walks and jogs as my leg got stronger. They even brought their dog, Maxim, along once or twice, which made them all laugh when he started growling at Quinn.

It was when I was sitting on the floor with my back leaning against Quinn one evening when everyone was around for food that I realized that I didn't think I could be much happier with my life. Everything was just that much brighter with Quinn by my side.

"What are you thinking?" Quinn asked after a few minutes of silence between us. He had been nuzzling into my hair and it felt nice.

I smiled and looked up. "Just that everything is going really great."

He raised his eyebrows. "And that's a problem why? It always should feel good when you're happy."

My smile grew bigger. "No," I said, grabbing him around the neck and pulling him to me. As he leaned down, I kissed him on the cheek. "Things are perfect for me right now. You make me feel so safe, protected and loved. Those feelings are what happiness feels like to me," I paused, and then blushed. "Well, they do anyway."

Quinn smiled down at me and pressed

a kiss to my forehead. A kiss that felt full of promise for this happiness to continue for as long as he had a say in my life.

Thank you for reading Jase and Quinn's story.
Continue the series with Gage, book 4 in Smokejumpers!

OTHER BOOKS BY EVE

Smokejumpers

Hawke

Cyrus

Jase

Gage

Federal Protection Agency

Mason

Rafe

Ryzen

Cooper

Noah

Damien

Federal Protection Agency Series

Omnibus Volume 1

EVE RILEY

Federal Protection Agency Series

Omnibus Volume 2

From The Edge Series

Shattered

Runaway

Jaded

Rescue

Hidden

Tormented

From The Edge Series: Books 1-3

From The Edge Series: Books 4-6

Gray Vale Pack Series

His Fate Mate

His Wounded Warrior

His Healing Heart

Gray Vale Pack Omnibus: Books 1-3

FOLLOW EVE...

Facebook Author Page

https://www.facebook.com/AuthorEveRiley/

Blog/Website

https://authoreveriley.blogspot.com/

Goodreads

https://www.goodreads.com/author/show/1
5007410.Eve_Riley

Bookbub

https://www.bookbub.com/authors/eve-riley

Twitter

https://twitter.com/AuthorEveRiley

LGBTQ+ Romance Books ARC Team

https://booksprout.co/author/25823/lgbtq-
romance-books

ABOUT THE AUTHOR

Born and raised in sun-drenched Australia, Eve Riley believes too much time spent at the beach is barely enough. Her partner says she's cute as a quokka or deadly as a taipan, depending on her blood-chocolate level.

She spends her nights writing bad boys in love, and her days wrangling the sweet boys she loves.

Milton Keynes UK
Ingram Content Group UK Ltd.
UKHW031703310124
437030UK00013BA/288